WENDY M. WILSON

Come to Grief

A Sergeant Frank Hardy Mystery

First edition

This book was professionally typeset on Reedsy.
Find out more at reedsy.com

Contents

Foreword

Many of the events in this novel are real; the SS *Tararua* did sink in April 1881, one of New Zealand's worst maritime disasters, and there was a gold robbery several months earlier from the same ship. The names and actions of real people in this book are as true as I could make them, in particular, this heroic group:

- Captain Garrard, who was later blamed for the disaster by an inquiry. He had been in a previous shipwreck where he acquitted himself heroically, and it was a shame he had to die in the way he did. He was only twenty-nine at the time of his death. His fiancée, Martha, married someone else a few years later.
- Antonio Miscalef, the head chef from Malta, who swam ashore and pulled others to safety. I could not discover anything about his later life.
- The Brunton family, Charles Brunton and his mother Jane Brunton who aided survivors at their own expense with both time and money. William Brunton, Jane's husband and Charles' father, died in June of that year. Jane Brunton was intended to be a minor character, but she swept into the plot full of energy, feeding survivors on the beach, organizing her kitchen, offering space to people to sleep, and riding to the rescue on a horse which I named

Nightingale after Florence, not the bird. The Brunton family really did donate the burial land and provide coffins for the dead at Tararua Acre. I hope I have painted them in the manner which they deserve.

- George Lawrence, the hero of the *Tararua* sinking, who swam ashore and went for help to a nearby outbuilding belonging to the Brunton family . He was a young man of twenty-two, and without him there would have been even fewer survivors. You can read about his later life here.
- Inspector Buckley and Detective Tuohy. Both these men went to the wreck to assist with the aftermath.

If you would like to follow the adventures of Frank and Mette on a map, click here.

NOTE: You may notice that I refer to the town of Bluff as Bluff Harbour, Bluff, and the Bluff. The Bluff is what New Zealanders call the town now, and also what they called it in 1881. If someone is a more formal speaker, or a second language speaker, like Mette, I have them say Bluff. Otherwise, I use the informal name, the Bluff. Bluff Harbour is the very large body of water that was one of New Zealand's earliest settlements.

1

A True British Seaman Dies at His Post

OFF THE COAST OF THE SOUTH ISLAND OF NEW ZEALAND: APRIL 28, 1881

It was not Captain Garrard's first shipwreck. But this time he knew the outcome would be different. No hard slog to safety to find help for his men, followed by accolades for his heroism. This time, he was a goner. Not only would he die, but the inquiry would most likely lay the blame at his feet. That he would not be alive to hear the conclusion did not make it easier to imagine.

Confronted with the reality of his impending doom, Captain Garrard stiffened his shoulders and prepared for what was to come.

He would protect the women and children for as long as possible, on the slim chance a ship would arrive to rescue them before they all drowned. At the very least, he offered hope. He was the youngest captain in the intercolonial service, and he was going to act accordingly.

The water, grey-green and implacable, had risen steadily for the past hour, engulfing the deck, and soaking his boots and trousers. The wind whipped at his clothing, pushing him towards the handrail on the fore deck, urging him to plunge into the icy depths below and finish it, like the purser and his wife.

As was the usual practice, he'd deployed lifeboats, but the sea was rough and one after another they had smashed against the hull or overturned, sinking as they hit the water. One had managed to reach the line of breakers and hold there; the men aboard had leapt into the surf and swum for it. Later, a shape crawled up the beach. Two people, perhaps. Hard to tell with the frozen pellets of salt water whipping against his eyeballs. Any man who made it ashore had been instructed to head for the nearest telegraph office and send for help. The captain prayed it would arrive in time, but knew in his heart it would not.

At first, he had not realized what a terrible dilemma faced him. He'd brought the passengers up on deck and asked the cook to serve them breakfast. They would be inconvenienced, merely, and there would be no negative talk about the incident afterwards.

But when the sky began to lighten to a dull grey and the group of seventeen people the doctor had gathered by the railing for safety were swept away after the railing collapsed, he understood he was not going to be able to get out of this fix. They were going to be picked off a few at a time by the monstrous beast that was the ocean, and he could do nothing

2

to stop it.

As night came and the situation became increasingly perilous, he'd taken the women and children to the smoking room for safety. When his own cabin next to the smoking room washed away, he'd brought the women and children up to the fore deck, telling them they'd be secure here until a ship arrived. They followed him blindly, clinging to the false hope he had given to them. What else was he to do?

With the arrival of darkness, it would not matter if a rescue ship came over the horizon this minute. They'd send the *Hawea* from Port Chalmers, probably. A good ship with an excellent captain and crew. If anyone could save the few who remained, it would be Captain Kennedy. But it would take hours to get here, and the swell was too great for rescue boats to reach them anyway.

The remains of one lifeboat still dangled from a davit; another was on the reef, broken in half; a third sat out at sea, the second officer at the helm, hoping to attract a passing ship. One boat had managed to make his way to the edge of the breakers before men had dived in and swum for it; that boat held the second mate, six sturdy crewmen who claimed they were good swimmers, Mr. Lawrence from steerage, and Sergeant Hardy, the chap who was after the gold robbers. And the brass polisher, of course. How foolish he had been to put the poor child in the lifeboat at the last minute, just because he claimed he could swim.

At least two of the men in the lifeboat had made it to shore, but others had not. On the beach, a cluster of settlers gathered around fires, waiting to help. Had they seen the two men who made it to shore? Would someone help them, point them in the direction of the nearest telegraph station?

A fair-haired woman clutching an infant in her arms slid across the deck in front of him, screeching. He caught her before she went over the edge and pulled her to her feet. She clung to his arm, staring at him, her eyes wide. "Are we going to die?"

"No, no. Help is on the way," he lied. "Hold the stanchion by the guardrail and keep your eyes closed. I'll let you know when the rescue ship arrives. Won't be much longer."

She obeyed, shivering and clutching the child to her breast. What a shame the two of them would die. An attractive young women and her baby — a little girl, he thought. He wondered where her husband was. Was he one of the dozens of men who had climbed into the rigging? Or was he pacing along the shore, hoping against hope his wife and child would be saved?

Even as he thought of the men above, a loud crack echoed through the night, and the foremast split away from its housing, taking the rigging and the men in it into the ocean, trapping some of them underneath. One of the women on the fore deck with him screamed her husband's name. "Jimmy. Jimmy." He was the man who had taken his child up with him and lashed them both there.

Heads bobbed in the water for a few minutes and then vanished. One or two might make it to the beach if they were strong swimmers. Or they might be swept out to sea, their bodies never to be found. The man lashed to the rigging with his child was certainly doomed.

He sighed, straightened his shoulders, and awaited his fate. Once he was in the water he would swim for the shore. Or drown. But he could not attempt to leave as long as a woman or child remained in his care. He could not embrace death, either, like the purser and his wife who had leapt off the aft deck together, sobbing, to a certain death.

The deck tilted sharply, and more women slid into the water, screaming as their heavy dresses and petticoats dragged them under. The surface of the water gleamed and frothed as the moon rose behind the clouds, and he watched with despair as a child, a young boy, thrashed around for several minutes before slipping below the surface.

The woman with the baby was still holding fast to the stanchion. As the boat cracked into two pieces and tipped slowly on its side, he locked eyes with her, knowing she thought the same as he did: we're both going to die.

He hit the water head first and went under, feeling himself pulled down by the sinking vessel. Down, endlessly down, until he could no longer hold his breath. At the last minute he rose to the surface again, popping up like a cork not far from the woman, the baby still in her arms, its eyes wide open, alive for now in the icy water.

The woman caught hold of a wooden gate and dragged herself and the baby onto it. He tried to swim towards her, but something was wrapped around his ankles. Kelp. He was caught in a patch of kelp. His strength waning, he pulled at the seaweed clinging to his legs, swallowing salt water all the while, unable to budge it. In the distance, the fire on the beach, beckoned him to safety. But he wasn't going to make it.

His last thought was of Martha, his fiancee in Melbourne, and the wedding they had planned. His friends had come to see him off from the wharf in Wellington, carrying champagne concealed in a flask, to congratulate him on his good fortune. Martha Buckhurst was the daughter of a wealthy man, and he had intended to leave the sea and join her father in his business. Sadness for the life he would never have overcame him. What would she think, his fiancee? Would she suffer? Would she find someone else?

He did not think again of the young, fair-haired woman with the baby in her arms, floating away on a wooden gate, taken by the hungry sea.

2

On Majoribanks Street

WELLINGTON, NEW ZEALAND. FOUR DAYS EARLIER.

Mette Hardy struggled downhill on Majoribanks Street trying to keep her skirt down and her umbrella up against impending rain, while steering her daughter Sarah Jane in her new woven-cane perambulator. Frank had purchased the pram from Mr. Tiller on Cuba Street, and although it was beautiful, it was almost impossible to manage on the steep Wellington hills.

The pram was a waste of money as far as she was concerned — money they didn't have. But Frank wanted his daughter to travel in style. As long as he had change in his pocket or credit at the bank his daughter would not lack for anything. Mette would have been perfectly happy to carry Sarah Jane on her back, as she'd seen Maori women doing. The babies always looked contented.

She crossed Roxburgh Street, the wheels of the pram bumping over the rutted cart tracks, and hit a pocket of salty wind whistling along the street from Oriental Bay. Her umbrella snapped upwards and turned inside out.

"Bugger." She checked to see if anyone had heard her swear. She'd learned to use words like that from Frank and knew she should try to control herself. Men were allowed to swear, especially when they'd been soldiers like Frank. She should swear in her native Danish so no one could understand what she was saying. Or in German, which was an excellent language for swearing. She shoved the broken umbrella into the pram, said some comforting words in Danish to Sarah Jane and carried on down the hill, hoping the rain would stop.

The damp wind slapped against her cheek and plastered strands of hair across her face; as she reached up to push her hair back in place, she stepped into a pothole and fell forward to her knees, wrenching her ankle painfully. The handle of the pram slipped from her grasp and the pram sped away. Heart pounding, she lifted her skirts and hobbled after it, knowing it was headed towards Kent Terrace where carts and drays and riders would be speeding along from both directions.

The pram bumped down the hill, gathering speed. Sarah Jane, whom Mette had propped up with pillows so she could see her mother, tossed from side to side in her nest looking surprised. Mette was gaining on her, but still not fast enough, when an elderly man stepped out of a gate and into their path. The next minute he was lying on the ground with Sarah Jane on top of him. The pram spun head over heels, landed back on its wheels, and continued on its way briefly before rolling out into the middle of the street and tipping on its side.

Stammering in shock about what had almost happened, she dragged the pram off the road before it could be smashed by a passing carriage.

"I'm so sorry. Are you hurt? The...the...*kinderwagen*... escaped from my hands, and..."

"Alles gut, danke," he answered as she helped him to his feet. She gave Sarah Jane a quick kiss and hug, and lifted her back into her pram. Sarah Jane smiled up at her, her wide brown eyes curious, wondering why she had been tossed from her carriage and into the arms of a strange man.

The strange man in question scooped up his hat from the ground and brushed off his suit with a handkerchief. He was short, with the self-confident posture of a professional man. His suit looked old, and was mended discreetly in several places, but had once been of good quality. His grey hair was combed back from his forehead, and he had a neat little Van Dyke beard.

"Good morning, madam," he said. "Did I hear you speaking German?"

"Did I? Sometimes I slip away from English when I'm upset, but I'm not German. I'm Danish. Well, Danish from Schleswig, so…"

"Ah, German then."

Mette did not reply. She had left Denmark when Germany had conscripted all the young men from her disputed home duchy into the Prussian army, and she preferred not to think of herself as German, although she spoke the language as well as she spoke Danish.

"Is your husband German as well? I know very few Germans in Wellington."

Mette nodded. "It's true there aren't many. But my husband is English. He came here as a soldier to fight in the land wars and decided to stay when they were over."

"A wise choice," said the stranger. "A person can make something of himself in this country."

"Have you made…" started Mette. "I mean, are you a

9

professional man?"

"Yes, indeed. I'm a professor at the new Wellington University. I teach modern languages." The professor took off his hat and bowed to Mette, clicking his heels together. "Professor Fritz Mann at your service."

"Pleased to meet you, Professor." Mette nodded at him, smiling. "I do some translation work from English into German, and from Danish into English." This claim was somewhat of an exaggeration as she had translated one book and a few letters, but she was eager to do more, especially now. The quarterly rent on the cottage was due in a few days and once she had paid that she'd be down to her last few pounds. A professor at the university might be a source of work, and of money.

Frank was arriving home today; at the moment he made a living procuring horses for the Armed Constabulary to use up at the Front; they brought in three pounds each. With luck, he'd bring a dozen this time. Last time he'd returned with five — barely enough to pay the interest on the bank loan, the wages of the manager of their horse farm, and the regular payment to Niall, their ward.

The professor stared at her, stroking his beard. "Do you have references for your translations?"

Mette hesitated. References? It hadn't occurred to her to ask anyone for those.

"Perhaps I could see your work," he said. "I need someone to do a translation for me. It's important that I publish something soon. The university senate requires that all professors publish, and I do have a large manuscript I brought with me from Germany. The senate would like something submitted before the end of the term. I believe they would be satisfied with a chapter or two if they knew more was coming."

She rummaged in her purse. "I have a page of my work here. It's a rough copy. I was using it for my shopping list."

Taking it from her, he scanned the three paragraphs on the page.

"This is excellent. Are you interested in working for me? I'll pay you two pounds per chapter…"

Mette was disappointed. That was half the amount Mrs. Halcombe had paid her, and chapter could take her a whole week.

"…and there are forty-five chapters, plus the abstract, of course."

"I could certainly try. Could I do one chapter for you so you can see a sample of my work?"

He looked away from her, and for a minute she thought he hadn't heard her. Then he turned back. "You could, but there is a little problem."

She waited.

"The full manuscript is in Dunedin at my old home. Someone has to collect it. I'd pay the fare, of course, and the cost of a night or two in a hotel."

Her heart sank. She was in no position to go all the way to the south of the South Island to fetch his papers by herself. And it wouldn't be worth Frank's time to go. He did better with the horses. Although, if he brought back some horses as well…that might be the solution.

"Perhaps my husband would go. I'm on the way to meet him now. Come with me and we'll find out."

The Armed Constabulary Depot bustled with activity. Soldiers in mufti loaded boxes of something onto carts — ammo by the look of it — encouraged by a sergeant with a booming voice. Off to the Front, no doubt. She was sick of all the talk about the Front, and the talk of war against the rebel Maori. She had come to New Zealand to escape a war, and hated knowing that fighting might happen in her new home.

Frank was in the yard talking to Colonel Roberts, the man to whom he reported. The colonel, a thin, stooping Englishman with a long, drooping moustache that ran into his beard on either side of his face, was doing his best to look down at Frank, who towered over him. As she always did, Mette felt a little flutter in her heart when she saw her handsome husband.

Frank saw her enter and excused himself, saluting the colonel who gave a langorous half-salute back, apparently too tired to complete the gesture.

He came over and picked up Sarah Jane, tickling her neck with his beard, which made her giggle and squirm. "How's my little girl?" He glanced at Mette. "I mean, how are both my girls."

"The pram ran away from me, and Sarah Jane almost got hurt," she said, not mentioning her ankle, which still throbbed.

He frowned. "You need to be more careful."

"Professor Mann saved her." She smiled at her new acquaintance. "He stepped in front of the pram and stopped it with his body."

Professor Mann cleared his throat. That wasn't exactly what had happened. He had stopped the pram by accident. But he said nothing to disabuse Frank, who clapped him on the shoulder. "How brave of you. Thank you."

"The professor is a teacher at the new university."

"Is that so?" Frank returned to pulling faces at Sarah Jane. Much to her surprise, he was the most doting of fathers, although only as long as the baby behaved. As soon as Sarah Jane began to act like a normal baby, he would hand her back to Mette.

She took a deep breath. Time to bring the conversation around to Dunedin, and the manuscript she had decided he was going to fetch for the professor.

"How many horses did you bring back this time?"

For a minute he ignored her question, focussing on pulling himself away from Sarah Jane who had grabbed his nose and was trying to latch on to it with her mouth. He freed himself and handed her the baby. "Three."

She was shocked. "Only three? How…?" She stopped, not wanting to mention their finances in front of the professor. Frank shrugged his apologies.

"I've been offered some work that might bring in good money," he said. "Colonel Roberts wants to send me further afield for another trip. More of an investigation."

"Where?" She hoped he'd say Dunedin, but did not expect that he would.

"The South Island. Lyttelton, Dunedin, Bluff Harbour, and back."

A miracle had taken place! Now she just had to persuade him to get the manuscript.

"Professor Mann has something he'd like us to do. He wants me to translate a book for him, but the manuscript is in Dunedin. I was hoping you could go…and now that you're going there anyway, you could get it."

He thought about it. "I'm going down by sea on the SS *Tararua*, and it docks in Dunedin to take on passengers, but I don't think I'd have time to get into town, pick up the manuscript, and get back to the ship before it left. And I have to keep an eye on some people, so I couldn't even guarantee I'd be able to leave the ship."

"There's a train from the port into town," said the professor. "Running on the hour. The house is in the centre of the city. You could get there and back to the ship very quickly."

Frank eyed him. She knew money was about to come up. "Would you pay for one fare?" he asked.

The professor nodded.

Frank turned to Mette. "Why don't you come with me on the *Tararua*? You could disembark in Dunedin and take the train into town, and then catch the train to the Bluff the next day. We'd arrive around the same time. My fare is already being covered with the job I'll be doing."

He had taken her breath away. To have an opportunity to see the South Island, which everyone said was the most beautiful place in the world, thrilled her. There was only one problem.

"What about the children?" In addition to Sarah Jane, they had an adopted son, a Maori boy who had been forced from his village with his brother and sister when the chief sold it to the government. His only relative was his grandmother, where he had been staying for the last week.

"Joey won't be back from Palmerston for another week. I'm sure his grandmother will keep him longer if necessary. I'll send her a telegram. And couldn't you leave Sarah Jane with someone? What about the girl you have coming in to help you, Bridget? Wouldn't she stay with her?"

Mette frowned. "She's much too young and unreliable." Leave Sarah Jane with Bridget? She wouldn't sleep a wink the whole time she was away. "No. I'll take her with me."

"You could take the pram…" said Frank.

Finally, a chance to rid herself of the bloody pram! Miraculous. "I'll carry her on my back." She tried not to smile. "Like the Maori women do, with a shawl wrapped around both of us and under her bottom. Then I won't have to push her around all the time."

The professor pulled out his pocket book. "I can give you an advance," he said to Mette. "Would five pounds cover everything?"

Before she could agree, Frank jumped in. "Five is a bit tight. Seven would probably be better. She'll need to stay in a hotel for the night, and pay for the train to the Bluff. And the fare on the *Tararua* is thirty shillings."

The professor opened his pocketbook and took out two bank notes. He handed them to Mette. "I'll write down the address for you. It's a boarding house, and the owner is Frau Mann, my wife. She'll give you my work. It's quite large, so you'll need to take a good-sized bag with you."

The professor left, after giving Mette both his own address in Wellington and the address of his wife in Dunedin. How strange that he had a wife living in another city; however, she had seen that kind of thing before. Perhaps they didn't love each other.

She and Frank walked along Buckle Street to Cuba Street and found a nice little cafe where they could get coffee and tea and light refreshments. He ordered both tea and coffee, with a plate of Mette's favourite date scones. She had intended to feed the baby when they arrived home, but for now kept her distracted with crumbs of scone covered in butter, which Sarah Jane licked off Mette's finger, her eyes half-closed in ecstasy.

"What's the job you have that takes you to the South Island?"

15

she asked, after she'd finished her coffee. "It's quite convenient for us, isn't it, both of us having something to do down there."

Frank spooned some warm, sweet, milky tea into Sarah Jane's mouth. "Remember that steamship robbery last year? Five gold ingots went missing from the *Tararua*, somewhere between Lyttelton and Melbourne."

Mette wiped some dribbled tea off Sarah Jane's chin and nodded. "Did they ever find who did it? I don't remember reading about an arrest."

"No, not even when the bank offered a reward of five hundred pounds. Now the reward is up to a thousand pounds."

Mette put her hand on her heart. "Oh my goodness. Do you have to find the gold to get the reward, or just the person who took it? A thousand pounds! Can you imagine how much that would help us?"

"The governor of the Bank of New Zealand told Colonel Roberts they've been following a group of crewmen for months. The entire crew was fired after the robbery, but there were several strong suspects. Recently, three of them booked passages on the ship for the next time it sails. Two leave from Wellington tomorrow, and a third boards in Dunedin the next day, all going to Bluff Harbour and then on to Melbourne."

"How can you follow three people at once?"

"They'll all be on the ship. I'm supposed to see if I can get one to turn on the other two. At this point the police are acting on the assumption that they're all in on it. They think the man boarding in Dunedin might be bringing the gold with him from a hiding place in town. I'll see if I can get to know one or the other of the men leaving from here. If I see a weakness in one, I'll try to get him to turn on his mates. There's a decent reward for getting one to talk, and if that leads to the recovery of the gold, then I believe I'd get the full shot."

"We'll be rich," said Mette. "How wonderful that will be. And I'll make something as well. Two pounds a chapter for translating forty-five chapters of Professor Mann's book. And a nice trip to the South Island as well. I've always wanted to see the South Island."

Frank squeezed her hand. "When we get to Bluff we can eat oysters together. Bluff is famous for oysters. We'll be able to afford to eat them every day after this."

3

Boarding the Tararua

The *Tararua* was docked at the railway wharf in Thorndon, one of the more squalid parts of town. To get to the ship, they had to pass by the infamous Thorndon Club, where a sixpenny membership bought a man the right to drink at any time of the day or night, and fallen women plied their trade for the same price.

Frank didn't want to go near the Club with Mette and Sarah Jane, but there was no other way to get to the wharf. As they neared the Club he took Mette's elbow. "Keep your eyes on the ground. It's pretty rough and I wouldn't want you to fall."

Mette, carrying a bag in either hand and Sarah Jane on her back, glanced at him, smiling. "Don't worry. I'll be careful."

As they reached the path in front of the club, a slovenly woman with a grubby white lace shawl draped provocatively around her shoulders leaned out from an upstairs window and coughed to get his attention. Frank glanced up, and she beckoned to him.

"Hey there, handsome. Want to leave your daughter and her wee one for a minute and come on up? Sixpence a pop."

"What did she say?" Mette had the end of the shawl holding Sarah Jane in a tight grip to keep it from unravelling.

"Nothing important." His daughter! He'd just turned forty-two and worried about his age compared to the much younger Mette, who was still in her twenties; at least he was fit and healthy and still had all his teeth and no grey hair — well, some in his beard. But he hadn't been mistaken for Mette's father before.

He was having second thoughts about taking Mette with him. If the wharf in Wellington was in a seedy part of town, might not the same be true of Dunedin? How would she manage without him? And what about Sarah Jane? He'd surprised himself with how much he adored his daughter, and worries about what might happen to the pair of them had begun to weigh on him. What had he been thinking, sending them off to a strange town alone, with Mette carrying Sarah Jane on her back like a peasant woman? And were babies that easy to carry around? Too late now to change his mind, but he would at least accompany them to the railway station when they disembarked in Port Chalmers, the port servicing Dunedin.

"We cross here." He took her elbow as they reached the Railway Hotel, guiding her past a gang of urchins who spent their days hanging around the station entrance. "Keep your eyes on the tracks. The wharf is behind the hotel."

Passengers were already climbing the gangplank although the ship wasn't sailing until high tide later that evening. A group of young men were celebrating their friend's impending nuptials; he was on his way to Australia to meet his bride, and the others had come to bid him farewell and express their approval.

"You'll forget all your friends in Wellington," one said,

slipping a flask from his vest pocket. He held it out to the bridegroom, a good-looking man of around thirty with dark hair and a neatly trimmed moustache. He wore a uniform Frank hadn't seen before, but he suspected the wearer was an officer on the ship. The would-be bridegroom shook his head and refused the proffered flask with a smile. "I'm on duty," he said, confirming Frank's suspicion. "And besides, as you know, I don't drink."

Nearby, a cluster of older men watched disapprovingly. Clergymen, Frank guessed. One held a bible to his chest while keeping an eye on the large bag by his feet to make sure no one ran off with it. The group had a long trip before them. The *Tararua* was on its way to Bluff, and then to Hobart and Melbourne, and most of the passengers were remaining on board after Bluff, including the three ex-crewmen Frank had been told to watch.

The *Tararua* sat at anchor, her dark blue hull rising and falling with the incoming tide.

"Quite the ship," Frank said. The bracing wind and the thought of travel invigorated him; he was going to enjoy this voyage. "Beautiful lines, and those engines…it will handle anything the sea throws at it. Plow right through the swells."

Mette nodded distractedly, ignoring the ship. He'd hoped to calm her nerves by engaging her with small talk about the ship. Knowing her fear of fast-moving trains, he assumed she'd be nervous about sea travel, even on a ship as safe as this one. The *Tararua* was a screw-driven steamer with powerful engines, part of the Union Steamship Company fleet, built originally for the Panama Line but now trading between Australia and New Zealand. Nothing to worry about. The ship was the safest of any of the hundreds of ships in the coastal waters of New

Zealand.

As they climbed the gangplank, he took Mette's bags from her so she could keep her balance by holding the ropes. Luckily, Sarah Jane was a quiet, contented baby. She had clamped her three teeth onto Mette's braid and was chewing appreciatively, ignoring the bustle of the ship. She was a bright little girl who seemed to have inherited her appearance from him and her intelligence from her mother, although what little hair she had was reddish blond and stuck straight up, rather than being dark and curly like his. He adored her.

A stewardess, a short, dark-haired woman dressed in the colours of the Union Line, greeted them at the top of the gangplank and took their tickets.

"Welcome aboard. Are you travelling with us to Melbourne?"

Frank smiled at her. "I'm off to Bluff. But my wife and daughter will disembark at Port Chalmers. I'll escort them to the railway station and return to the ship. Will that be a problem, Miss…?"

"Aitken," said the stewardess. "Jennie Aitken. No, of course it won't be a problem. I'll make sure the purser knows."

"Is the captain on board yet? I need to speak with him on an important matter."

"That's him on the wharf." Miss Aitken pointed to the group of men celebrating the departure of the bridegroom. "Captain Garrard. This will be his final voyage. He's getting married when he reaches Melbourne and starting a new life. I believe he'll be working for his father-in-law."

"I suppose he's been the captain of the *Tararua* for a while?"

She shook her head. "Only for a few months. After the gold robbery last year, the entire crew was fired, including Captain Muir. Captain Garrard was assigned to us then. His first command, I believe."

Frank could feel Mette beside him, swaying with the movement of the ocean, holding the rail with both hands. He took her by the elbow. "I'll take my wife to our quarters and come back up on deck. Would you tell the captain I'd like to speak with him?"

She smiled politely, not wanting to accommodate him too easily. "Could I tell him what it's about? He'll be busy once he comes aboard."

"It's a police matter."

"And you are?"

"Sergeant Hardy. Sergeant Frank Hardy."

"I'll tell him to expect you." She glanced down at the passenger list in her hand and looked back at Frank, still smiling. "You're on the lower deck in an intermediate cabin. Number 6C. The water closet is at the end of the passageway. You're not sharing with anyone — just the two of you and the baby. Dinner and drinks are available in the saloon, or you can take your evening meal back to your cabin if you wish." She gestured over her right shoulder. "Take the ladder by the saloon. Give the captain an hour and then check the wheelhouse or the smoking room beside it."

Their cabin on the lower deck was tiny, with two sets of bunks, only one of which had blankets and pillows. There was no porthole or private bath — just a wash stand in the corner with a ewer and basin on top and a plain white chamber pot hidden behind a curtain underneath. Frank was unable to stretch to his full height, and there was nowhere to sit, other than on the lower bunks. It reminded him of the cell he'd been confined to in the upper reaches of the Whanganui River two years earlier.

Mette sat on the lower bunk with blankets. "Sarah Jane and I will sleep here. You can take the upper bunk. Will you fit?"

"Of course I will." He patted the mattress on the upper bunk, noticing how lumpy it was. He'd fit if he slept with his knees crushed against his chest, but he was used to that. He'd been hoping to share the lower bunk with Mette, although he'd have even less room if they did. "Can't Sarah Jane sleep in the upper bunk?"

Mette took off Sarah Jane's bonnet and put it on the bed, smoothing her daughter's hair. "Of course not. You know how much she wriggles. She'd fall out of bed and hurt herself. Although I suppose I could prop her up with something. No. Best she sleeps with me. I have to feed her and change her now, so you go ahead and talk to the captain." She opened one of her bags and took out a fresh cotton napkin and the small wooden box of burnt flour that she carried to sooth the baby's rashes, setting them beside a book she'd brought with her to read while she fed Sarah Jane. Another one by her favourite author, *Hard Times* by Charles Dickens. She'd left her current darling, *Bleak House*, at home, saying it was too heavy to carry.

Mette picked up the baby and the book and gave Frank a look. He escaped to the upper deck to see the captain. He knew when he was in the way.

The captain was in the wheelhouse deep in discussion with the first officer. He turned when Frank tapped on the door frame. "Yes?"

"Frank Hardy. I asked Miss Aitken to tell you I wanted to speak with you."

"Ah, yes. Sergeant Hardy. What can I do for you? Miss Aitken didn't say."

23

"The Armed Constabulary sent me to follow three suspected gold robbers."

"Again?" The captain frowned. "This ship was robbed last year. Does the Constabulary think someone intends to rob us again? I don't believe we're carrying any gold, although we do have a shipment of silver, and the mail, of course."

"This is about the last robbery," said Frank. "Three crewmen from that trip purchased tickets for this one. We think they may be picking up the ingots somewhere and taking them to Melbourne."

Captain Garrard shook his head. "Hard to believe…everyone has been investigated very thoroughly. Do you have the names of the men you're following?"

Frank pulled a piece of paper from his pocket. "The first is Robert Hinton. He was a steward I believe."

"The American," said the captain. "The Melbourne police had him under surveillance for months. I heard he joined the *Otway*, on the Western Australia run. He's on the ship now, you say?"

"He bought a ticket, or so I was told."

"Tall, dark red hair. Yankee way of talking. I saw him in Melbourne a couple of times. He doesn't know me though. Who else?"

"William Sampson. He was part of the crew."

"Less likely to have done it then. Access to the key was an important feature of the robbery, or so I heard. I don't know him." He turned to his first officer who was charting a course at the map table. "How about you, Mr. Maloney? William Sampson sound familiar?"

The first officer scratched his cheek with his pencil. "I think so. We were on the *Hawea* together at one point. Average

24

height and heavyset. Dark hair with mutton chops lining his jaw, a surly expression at all times. Come to think of it, I believe I saw the two of them boarding together earlier. I didn't think anything of it. I should have, I suppose."

Frank consulted his list. "The third man is William McNab. Another steward. He's not on board yet; he's boarding in Port Chalmers."

The captain and the first officer glanced at each other. "Never heard of him," said the first officer.

"I'll ask Miss Aitken to point him out to you after he boards," said the captain. "But I don't recognize the name. Are you sure he was one of the crew?"

"His name is on my list," said Frank. "What did you say about access to keys?"

"The company had a special strongroom built for gold, in the stern of the ship under the saloon. Only two people had a key. Officials of the Bank of New Zealand brought the gold on board in Port Chalmers; eleven boxes valued at five thousand pounds each. When the ship reached Queen's Wharf in Melbourne and officials came on board to carry it off, there were only ten. One had been stolen."

"Were either of the two men with keys considered suspects?"

"One of them was Captain Muir. That was why he lost his job — and his reputation. He runs a hotel in Melbourne now. I've spoken to him. He seems like a decent chap. I believe he was cleared. But after the gold went missing, police discovered that a year earlier one of the keys to the strongroom had disappeared from its spot in the bar room. Something should have been done at the time, of course, but it wasn't. And the lock wasn't changed, either. The police believe the robber was waiting for the right opportunity. With that many boxes it was hard to tell at a glance that one was missing. And the ship doesn't often carry that much gold. A steward would be more likely to hear there was a large amount of gold on that trip than a crew member."

"Would you like to see the bullion room, Sergeant?" asked the first officer. "Give you a feel for the situation? There's no gold there at the moment, just some silver bullion."

Frank followed the first officer down into the bowels of the ship and through the crew's quarters. As they passed the ladder to steerage he saw two men huddled by the emergency life jackets: one was tall with dark red hair that ran down the side of his face into a pair of bushy whiskers, the other was short, stocky, and dark-haired. The first officer caught his eye and gestured slightly with his head.

Frank nodded at the men and said, "Good evening," which he would have done even if they weren't suspects in a gold robbery. He felt them watching him as he continued down the passageway to the bullion room. Were they planning to rob the ship again? He'd have to keep an eye on the strongroom, just in case. No use accepting the job of watching two suspects and letting them rob the ship again. No one was going to give him a reward if that happened.

The first officer showed him the door to the bullion room. He tried the handle and attempted to push the door open with his shoulder. The door didn't budge. It was a sturdy door made of heart of kauri, fortified with iron bars. No one could get into this room without a key. He unlocked the door, which opened to a small dark room with a metal locker on one side.

"Was the gold in the locker?" Frank asked.

"On any other trip it would have been, but because there

were so many boxes, they piled them in the corner. The captain and the first officer checked it every hour, but eleven boxes suddenly reduced to ten - that would have been hard to see. I heard they took one from the back of the pile so it was less apparent."

He returned to the cabin to find Mette, her hair brushed and braided, ready to go to the saloon for dinner. Sarah Jane was asleep on the lower bunk, propped in place by a pillow and Mette's Gladstone bag.

Mette touched Sarah Jane's head gently. "She'll sleep for the next four hours. We can leave her for an hour. I'd like a tour of the ship, and then I'd like to have tea."

Climbing the ladder to the upper deck, he heard someone come up from steerage and fall in behind him on the ladder. He turned to greet the person: Robert Hinton, the red-haired American, stared back at him, a faint sneer on his face. He turned back and continued to the saloon. Something in the way Hinton had looked at him was worrying. Did he suspect something? Had someone recognized him and talked to Hinton? Or worse, had someone already warned Hinton that an investigator was on the ship?

4

Mette in Dunedin

After a restless night fighting off queasiness from the movement of the ship, and a difficult day pacing the deck with a
fretful baby, Mette was feeling out of sorts when they docked
at Port Chalmers at four o'clock in the afternoon. The view
that met them was not encouraging. The day was chilly, and
a sharp wind whipped across the railway tracks leading out
to the wharf. Old newspapers and dead leaves were piled in
front of the transit shed where an elderly man huddled by the
door, floppy hat resting almost on his shoulders, hugging his
coat around knees to keep himself warm.

They had managed to spend some time together, but not
long enough to satisfy either of them. After wedging the
sleeping Sarah Jane in the top bunk with pillows and coats,
they squeezed into the lower bunk, laughing quietly as they
manoeuvred awkwardly in the short, narrow bed. But before
they could find a comfortable position, the baby heard her
parents beneath her and began to whimper. Frank rolled on
his side, propped himself up on one elbow, and banged his
head against the ladder to the upper bunk.

"Damn."

Mette shushed him as he rubbed the back of his head, but too late. The whimpers turned to sobs.

She climbed over him and out of the bunk. She knew he would be disappointed; they hadn't been together for over a week, and the baby wasn't helping. But she was unable to leave Sarah Jane by herself, crying.

Frank rolled out of the bed, shook his head regretfully as he accepted the inevitable, and climbed into the upper bunk. "I hope the bed in the hotel in the Bluff is more comfortable than this. I can barely fit up here."

She snuggled with Sarah Jane, talking softly to lull her to sleep. Finally, the baby drifted off, her thumb slowly slipping from her mouth. Mette's arm was trapped in an awkward position and went to sleep. She was unable to move and wished she was rocking from side to side and not end to end. She had forgotten how much that movement had upset her stomach on the ship from Copenhagen to New Zealand. In the upper bunk, Frank's snores echoed around the cabin. In spite of his complaints, he was able to sleep anywhere. She envied him. Since Sarah Jane's birth she had not had one single full night's sleep.

Sarah Jane woke early and Mette took her up to the fore deck to watch as the ship passed through the heads and entered Otago Harbour, which was bathed in a fine mist. The purser and his wife were enjoying the sight as well, discussing the way the light reflected off the water, and how they planned to paint the scene when they anchored in Bluff Harbour. She listened to them talk, and thought about the art book she had translated for Mrs. Halcombe. She hoped Professor Mann's book would be half as interesting.

She could see the lights of Port Chalmers in the distance and was entranced by the beauty of the morning. But she was forced to return to her cabin when the mist turned to rain and the fore deck became too slippery to walk on carrying a baby. By then, the purser and his wife had already gone below. Mr. Jones had smiled at her as he left. "No rest for the wicked."

"He has to serve second breakfast this morning," his wife had explained to Mette. "Perhaps we'll see you and your daughter in the dining room."

With the ship finally tied snuggly against the wharf, they trudged down the gangplank, stepping aside briefly to let a young woman walk by on her way up. The woman held a baby on her right hip, slumped forward like a bag of corn; she glanced at Mette and Sarah Jane, not responding to Mette's friendly smile. As she passed them, she hoisted the baby from one hip to the other, causing it to whimper, and tucked her own straw-coloured hair behind her ear, her bracelet slapping against the baby's head. Mette longed to take the poor baby and put her against her mother's shoulder. If she carried Sarah Jane that way, her baby would soon make her displeasure clear.

A man of about thirty with similar light-coloured hair followed several feet behind the young woman, not talking to her and not helping her. He had the look of a soldier: upright, squared shoulders, striding up the gangplank. The pair were alike enough to be brother and sister and must be travelling together. Mette wondered where they might be going, the three of them; she was interested in people's stories. Why was the young woman with straw-coloured hair with her brother, if that's what he was? Where was the baby's father? And why wasn't her brother helping her to board?

Frank said a curt, "Good afternoon," to the couple as each one squeezed by him on the narrow gangplank. The woman ignored him, but the man nodded back, and raised his hand in a half-salute, as if he recognized Frank as an ex-soldier.

As they continued down the gangplank, Frank turned to Mette, looking relieved. "I'm happy to see you're not the only woman travelling with a baby."

She could tell that having the baby on the trip was weighing on him. She knew him well and was sure he was sorry he had encouraged her to go off on her own with Sarah Jane. Strangely, the companionship of Sarah Jane was a comfort to her. It was only the second time she'd been anywhere alone, and she was unsure of her herself. Sarah Jane needed frequent feeding and changing, but she also provided smiling approval, especially when she was being fed; during those times, she stared at Mette as if the feeding nourished her both physically and emotionally. It was the most wonderful emotion Mette had felt since the day she met Frank, and it gave her courage.

She forced herself to seem cheerful as he escorted her to the train, Sarah Jane once more strapped to her back, but grizzling; as usual, her mood mirrored Mette's.

"I can't wait to see Dunedin. Professor Mann said it's a beautiful town."

"Don't see too much of it," he said, with an unconvincing casualness. "Find yourself a decent boarding house and stay in your room for the night. It's cold out."

He helped her on to the Dunedin train, which was sitting at the station waiting for passengers from the *Tararua*, and then kissed her goodbye, hugged Sarah Jane, and left in the direction of the ship.

As soon as he was out of sight, Sarah Jane's grizzle changed

31

to a wail. Mette took the baby from her back and walked up and down the aisle rubbing her back, but nothing seemed to help.

A man boarding the train glared at her as he shoved his bag — a brown leather Gladstone bag identical to the one she carried — onto the rack above his seat. "Can't you keep that blasted baby quiet?"

Mette stuck her little finger in Sarah Jane's mouth. "She's just a baby," she said. "She's had a hard night on the ship and she's sleepy and hungry."

"Aren't we all bloody sleepy and hungry?" he said. "You don't see me crying about it."

She walked away from him and stared out at the platform. Bugger him. How dare he criticize her beautiful little girl. She thought she'd seen him on the ship somewhere — she recognized that ugly red hair and long, narrow face framed with red whiskers. By the way he had said can't - more like cant - she thought he might be an American or a Canadian. Not that she had anything against Americans or Canadians, but she disliked the idea of someone from another country criticizing her little New Zealander. The cheek of him!

The trip into Dunedin was rapid. The train raced along billowing dark clouds of smoke, the wheels making a hypnotic clickety clack sound. Mette had always been nervous about trains, but she felt safe on this one. Sarah Jane fell asleep in her arms, and when the time came to leave the train, she squatted down and lifted her bags, holding the baby in place against her chest. A conductor was waiting on the platform and took her bags from her and held her elbow as she negotiated the steep steps without being able to see them.

"Thank you very much. Oh, what are you…?"

The red-haired American had appeared from nowhere and picked up one of her bags.

"That's my bag," she said. It was the brown leather Gladstone bag she had borrowed from Frank, because it was large enough for a manuscript.

"I don't think so," he said. "It's mine. It's one I've had for years and I recognize it. It isn't a bag that a lady would carry, either." He walked away with it in his hand. The conductor ran after him and grabbed him by the shoulder. "The lady handed it to me from the carriage. I saw her coming along the aisle with it. Where was yours?" He took hold of the handle and pulled, but the American resisted.

"She was sitting near me. She got confused by that bloody baby of hers. Mine was above my seat. I hopped out to have a smoke and it was gone when I came back."

The conductor gestured to the back of the train. "We took off some bags that didn't seem to have owners. They're down there. Check before you try to take this lady's bag from her." He gained control of the bag and put it by his feet. "I'll keep it here until you come back."

The American glared at Mette. "Don't leave with that bag." he said. "Or there'll be hell to pay." He strode off to the rear of the train. They saw him pick a bag from a pile and leave without saying anything to them or offering an apology.

"A real gentleman," said the conductor. "He must have something important in his bag. Do you need help getting somewhere? I can get you a porter for sixpence."

She nodded. She could afford sixpence, just this once.

He woke the old man sleeping by the transit shed door and thrust Mette's bags at him.

"This is old Jack. Get up Jack. The lady needs a hand with her bags." The old man tottered to his feet, rubbing his eyes. He was not what Mette had expected when she heard the word porter, but he would have to do.

"Give him his sixpence when he gets you to where you're going," the conductor advised. "Where is that, anyway?"

"I'm not sure...I need to find a hotel or rooming house. Something inexpensive but nice."

"Moray Place," he said. "That's the street with the most reasonably priced rooming houses. It's an uphill walk so you'll be glad of the help. Jack, take this lady to Mrs. Bentley's on Moray Place." He took out his watch. "Dinner is in thirty minutes, so be quick. You'll like Mrs. Bentley. She cooks a nice joint with lots of roasted potatoes and carrots. And the beds are soft. She'll be happy to see a woman with a baby. Loves babies, she does."

Her mouth watering in anticipation, Mette followed Jack through a maze of streets and up a long stretch of hill. They circled a stone church sitting on a grassy knoll, with a huge spire that reached towards heaven. She took note of it, thinking it would help her find her way back to the train station tomorrow. The train to Bluff left at ten the next day, and she had already purchased her ticket. She needed to pick up the manuscript before she caught the train as well.

They arrived in front of a three storey house with a cheerful red door and a pot of blue cornflowers on the step. She gave Jack his sixpence and knocked on the door. As she waited for someone to answer, her mood was ruined when she glimpsed the red-haired American entering a house a few doors down. He was carrying his bag — the one like hers — but gave no indication that he had seen her.

34

Mrs. Bentley did love babies. She ushered Mette in to her private parlour and insisted she have a cup of tea while she waited for the dinner bell. Mette took the time to feed Sarah Jane, hoping no one would come in. It was so difficult finding a secluded place when you travelled, and people often reacted in an unpleasant way when they noticed her feeding Sarah Jane. Even at home, Frank left the room when she fed the baby, as if there were something unnatural about it. He'd suggested she hire a wet nurse, but she had dug in her heels and refused to consider it. She suspected it was the English way. In Denmark, wet nurses existed mainly to help in cases where a mother had died, or a woman did not have enough milk, but New Zealand observed the ways of the old country.

The dinner bell rang and she buttoned up her dress and went to get dinner, thinking that all she needed now was to find the American sitting at the table.

However, Mrs. Bentley was presiding over a group of young men all dressed in smart grey suits. Travelling salesmen, she guessed. One young man jumped up and pulled up a chair for her.

Mrs. Bentley moved a newspaper from a large armchair. "Put your baby here while you eat your dinner. We can prop her up with cushions. She'll be quite safe."

Another young man popped up and helped her wedge Sarah Jane in the armchair. "What a pretty little girl," he said. "Better keep her safe if you don't want her to be stolen away."

Mette's heart dropped to the pit of her stomach. "Stolen... what do you mean...why...?"

"Don't listen to John." Mrs. Bentley glared at the offending young man. "It isn't anything for you to worry about."

He frowned. "She should know. She might want to be extra

35

careful. The police have no idea why it happened."

"Know what? Did something bad happen?"

"A baby was kidnapped from the North Ground yesterday, during a cricket match. It was in the paper this morning. The nursemaid was rocking the baby in its perambulator while watching her young man play. She was approached by a man she didn't know, who asked her the score. She turned away for no more than a minute. When she turned back the baby was gone."

"Did anyone see anything? Wouldn't someone notice a baby being taken from a pram?"

"Several people saw a woman pick up the baby and walk away quickly, but they assumed it was her mother," said John. "She was wearing nice clothes and jewelry and didn't appear to be the type of person who would steal a baby. Everyone thinks the man was an accomplice. They'd never seen either of them before, and the descriptions are so varied that the police are having trouble narrowing down whether they were young or old, short or tall, or wearing dark or light clothing. The woman had a shawl over her head that hid her face. And it happened right as Howlison of the Caledonians hit a four, and the audience was cheering madly and watching him take his run."

"Is the North Ground far from here?" asked Mette. Her heart was starting to pound. She wanted to take Sarah Jane and hide in the bedroom.

"Don't you worry, it's…" Mrs. Bentley began.

But John was determined to spill the whole story. "It's under a mile away. But the baby had a nursemaid, so I'm sure she came from a wealthy family. There's no reason anyone would want to kidnap your baby."

"I heard it was the father," said one of the other men.

"Nah," said John. "It was about money. It always is with these rich people."

Mette had intended to take Sarah Jane for a walk after dinner to pick up Professor Mann's manuscript, but what with the kidnapping and her fear of running into the American, she was considering taking Frank's advice and shutting herself in her room with the door locked. But she had to get the manuscript tonight to give her time to catch the train tomorrow. If she missed it and Frank arrived in Bluff before them, he would worry. She could send a telegram, of course, but she'd never sent one before and had no idea how to go about it or how soon Frank might receive it. No, the only solution was to get it tonight.

"Does anyone know where Stuart Street is?" she asked. "Is it anywhere near the North Ground?"

"It's in the direction of the Ground, but not far from here," said Mrs. Bentley. "Do you want to go to Stuart Street?"

Mette nodded. "I have to pick up a manuscript for a professor. But after hearing about the kidnapping, I'm too nervous to go out."

"Well," said Mrs. Bentley. "I think it's only fair that John escorts you. John?"

John looked shamefaced. "I'm sorry Mrs. Hardy. I didn't mean to scare you. Of course I'll take you there. We can leave as soon as we've finished our pudding. Jam tart tonight, isn't it Mrs. Bentley?"

5

On the Reef

Frank stopped on the gangplank to take a last look back at the train, wondering if it was too late to stop Mette from leaving. A shaft of sunlight had broken through the clouds and shone through the train window, glinting off her golden hair. She was holding Sarah Jane against her cheek and rubbing her back. The sight both warmed and terrified him. What if she got into trouble? What had he been thinking? He could fetch her now and they could pick up the manuscript on the return voyage. But while he was worrying about it, the train moved slowly away from the platform.

He turned reluctantly and continued up the gangplank. For now, he would focus on the job. He would ask Miss Aitken, collecting tickets at her post, if she'd seen William McNab. His third suspect should have boarded the ship by now, and Miss Aitken should be able to describe him.

However, her place had been taken by the purser, who was collecting tickets and directing passengers to their cabins.

The purser reached out a hand to Frank. "Ticket please."

"I gave it to Miss Aitken when I boarded in Wellington. I

was seeing my wife and daughter to the train. I mentioned it to Miss Aitken. I thought she'd be here."

"Ah, yes. Sergeant Hardy. She did tell me about you. Go ahead."

He leaned around Frank. "Next, please."

Frank stayed where he was. "Miss Aitken was going to point someone out to me."

The purser straightened himself. "She didn't mention that. Who?"

Frank hesitated, reluctant to tell anyone else why he was on board.

"William McNab," he said finally, without elaborating.

The purser shrugged. "We're in Dunedin. They're all Scots here, and at least half of them have names beginning with Mc. Can you tell me anything else? Was he travelling alone? Young? Old? Tall? Short?"

"Are you going to be long, Mr. Jones?" said a quavery voice. "I'll need to sit down soon."

Behind him, an elderly woman in deep mourning was fanning herself with a lace handkerchief, her face white with fatigue.

"I'm sorry." Frank stepped aside. "Go ahead, I'll wait."

"Tell you what." The purser took the woman's ticket and directed her to a cabin on the saloon deck. "Why don't you ask Miss Aitken in the morning? She's resting now, because she's on first breakfast at six bells. She'll ask passengers their names as she seats them. If you're at breakfast early she can give you the nod when this McNab fellow enters the dining room. I won't be there. My wife is on this trip with me and I requested the second sitting so we could get up early and see the harbour as the sun rose. We enjoy painting watercolours

39

of the ocean, both of us."

"I'll do that. Thank you." He'd been expecting to know the identity of the third suspect by now, and to begin the process of finding the weak link. He could start tomorrow, of course; in the meantime, with a day and a half before they anchored in Bluff Harbour, he could at least check on Hinton and Sampson to see what they were up to.

He started with the upper deck, walking from end to end, past the wheelhouse and the smoking room next to it, and finally the saloon. There, a young man was busy setting boxes of cutlery on each table, preparing for the morning meal. The tables were already covered with cream-coloured linen table cloths, with plates stacked to one side in bolted-down cages to keep them from smashing when the weather got rough.

William Sampson sat at the bar staring into space. He had a mug of beer in one hand and a shot glass in front of him on the bar; he looked like he was settling in for the night. The red-haired American, Hinton, was not with him.

Frank took a seat near Sampson and ordered himself a pint of Dog's Head. The local stuff was good, but he was still partial to imported brews.

He gulped down half of the beer, and tapped the bar to catch the attention of the barman, "How soon are we casting off?"

The barman was polishing a glass he'd immersed briefly in a bowl of grey water covered in soap scum. "As the tide turns. In an hour or so." He glanced pointedly at Sampson. "The bar closes at seven, before we pass through the heads and things get rough. I need time to secure the glasses and bottles and to clean up."

Frank tossed down the rest of his pint. "In that case I'll have another. What's good?" He turned towards Sampson. "What're you drinking?"

Sampson shrugged.

"I'll have the same as him." Frank leaned forward to make sure Sampson could see him. "Can I get you one?"

Sampson shrugged again and pushed his glass forward.

"Gimme me an East India Pale Ale. And a whisky chaser, same as before."

The barman raised one eyebrow at Frank, who nodded. "Same for me." He'd been trying to stick to beer, but a whisky chaser sounded inviting. It would help him sleep. He had a feeling he was going to have trouble sleeping without Mette.

He downed the second beer and the whisky, and nodded to the barman. "Same again, please." He felt good. It had been a while since he'd had a drink.

Sampson was slumped forward, his eyes half-closed. "Give me another," he said, without offering to pay for Frank's drinks. "Beer and a whisky chaser again."

"Disembarking in Bluff, are you?" asked Frank. He was confident he could drink anyone under the table, but Sampson could go under the table any minute; no point in waiting to begin questioning him.

Sampson nodded. "Going to Australia. Me and my mate. Looking for work."

"Ship's crew, are you?"

Sampson eyed him suspiciously. "What makes you ask that?"

"Just a guess," said Frank. "Gold miners, then?"

Sampson tossed back his beer and pushed away from the bar. "None of your bloody business."

"He's crew." The barman watched as Sampson stumbled from the saloon. "I recognize him from the *Hawea*. I worked the bar on the *Hawea* for a couple of years."

41

Frank was feeling pleased with himself as he returned to his cabin, but remembering that Mette and Sarah Jane had gone dampened his spirits. He removed his boots and money belt and squeezed into the lower bunk fully dressed so he could get to the saloon early.

The beer and whisky sent him into a deep sleep, and, for the first time in months, into dreadful nightmares. His brother again, and that head dangling from the pole by its hair. He was on horseback for some reason, on Copenhagen, the horse he'd had to shoot after she swallowed poison. They were swaying from side to side, and he knew it was the movement of the ocean although the dream seemed horribly real. He tried to rescue his brother, knowing it was too late, spurring Copenhagen across the river between the camp and the head on the pole, his rifle raised to shoot; half way across the river Copenhagen disappeared from beneath him and he felt himself drop into the water.

He awoke with a jolt to find he'd fallen head first out of the lower bunk. He dragged himself up and separated himself from the bedding, trying to dispel the vestiges of the nightmare and the emotions that came with it.

Outside his cabin, he heard the muffled sounds of voices and people running. A woman screamed in terror, and children were crying. He stood, nervous, and looked in the upper bunk, forgetting for a minute that Mette and Sarah Jane had already disembarked.

But the floor beneath him had tilted noticeably. Something wasn't right.

His money belt was hidden under the mattress; he strapped it around his middle, tucked his shirt into his trousers, stepped into his boots, and wrenched open the cabin door.

The passageway was in darkness, the gaslights having been extinguished for the night, but someone had struck a safety match; in the flickering light he could see the terrified faces of women still in nightdresses and men holding small children. They were waiting to climb the ladder. Men from steerage jostled at the top of the ladder from steerage, anxious to join the queue. All movement had come to a stop, blocked by an older man who was trying to shove a large suitcase up the ladder to the upper deck, cutting off their escape. As Frank bounced between the wall and the bulkhead, trying to reach the ladder, hands reached out and grabbed the suitcase, throwing it to the ground.

"Don't be bloody stupid, mate," said one man as he elbowed his way forward. "You'll kill us all."

Once the families and the men from steerage were swallowed up into the dark above, he followed them. The ladder leaned with the listing of the ship, making his ascent difficult.

He was met at the top by near total darkness. Sunrise must be hours away. He felt his way along the upper deck, which was awash with seawater and tilting dangerously to port, slipping several times towards the rail, barely stopping himself from taking a header over the side.

In the gloom he saw the elderly woman in mourning who had been behind him as he boarded, wedged with her back against the gangplank gate, her arms clawing the air like the legs of a cast sheep. He let himself slip down against the rails again and dragged himself towards her. He was feet away when the gate broke open with a loud crack and flew off into the darkness. Her nails scraped against the deck for a few seconds, and then she disappeared without a sound.

He held the railing and leaned over, scanning the surface

of the ocean, but could see nothing — just the broken gate bobbing beside the ship. Less than a mile away, a heavy mist covered the land. At the prow of the ship, surf broke over a line of rocks and splashed upward. They were stuck on a reef, although at least the ship was still be in one piece.

As he neared the wheelhouse, he passed clusters of passengers standing quietly and fearfully, waiting for instructions. The captain was braced in the door to the wheelhouse, bellowing above the incoming waves at a man sitting on the deck, his leg twisted beneath him. A grizzled crewman squatted beside him holding him in place with oil-covered hands.

"You *know* what to do, Munro. Reverse the engines and get the damn ship off the reef. We'll break up if we stay here."

The man on the deck grimaced in pain. "I tried sir. I got your orders to reverse the engines. But when I did the propeller broke. The water's coming up fast in the boiler room. The hull must have been breached."

"Can you get down in there at all? Make repairs?"

"No sir. And the hatch fell on me when I was coming up to ask for instructions. My leg's broken. I need the surgeon."

"Find the ship's doctor," the captain said to the crewman beside the engineer.

"What can I do?" asked Frank.

The captain was breathing hard, not panicking, but obviously aware he was in serious trouble. "We're on the Otara Reef. I thought we were further out. I was asleep and came up to tell Henry to steer directly towards Bluff Harbour. There isn't a lighthouse on Waipapa Point and I thought we were well out from the reef. Stupidity!"

Frank hung on to the door jamb to stop the water dragging him over the side of the ship. Clearly, the captain was afraid it was his fault. He would know inquiries were always called to assign blame, and that the findings of such an inquiry would follow him forever.

"Are we sinking?"

"Not yet, but the boiler room's filling up and we can't move. The propeller's broken and the rudder's unshipped. I'm going to start lowering lifeboats. Can you swim? I need some strong men to get ashore and go for help."

Frank nodded. "I can swim. But you'll need to send several men to make sure at least one makes it to shore. What are our odds, do you think?"

"I can swim," said a slim young man with short, curly hair and the beginnings of a moustache. I was school champ and I've swum in the surf lots of times. The name's Lawrence. George Lawrence."

"Alright. The two of you, and I'll send the second mate and some crewmen with you. But grab the ropes first, Hardy, and help lower the boat. Mr. Maloney, you're in charge. Get these two off in the first boat, then go yourself in the second one."

"What about you, sir?" asked Maloney. "Will you take charge of a boat? You're a strong swimmer."

The captain shook his head, his face grim. "No. I'll stay until the end."

As he strained on the ropes, Frank was grateful he'd been running up and down Mount Victoria with a load of bricks on his back whenever he'd had the opportunity. His back and arms felt strong as he took most of the weight at one end of the lifeboat beside George Lawrence. But the angle of the ship proved too much for the crew, who released the other end too soon. The boat dropped from its davits, plunged beneath the surf and popped up filled with water. It hung there, smashing against the hull, becoming more useless with each hit.

They did better with the second boat, holding it above the surface of the water long enough to allow the men to scramble down the rope ladder before dropping it all the way in. George Lawrence went first, followed by two of the crew. As he swung into the lifeboat, Frank heard the captain tell someone to climb after him.

"Go ahead, lad. One more small one won't make any difference."

A boy of about eleven or twelve shinnied down the rope after Frank, grinning, unafraid. "My dad taught me to swim."

"Is your father on the ship?"

He shook his head. "My dad's at Bluff Harbour He works on the wharf there. I'm the brass polisher. My dad knew the last captain and he got me this job."

Frank eyed the boy's frail body. What had made Captain Garrard think this boy would fare well in the lifeboat? He was so thin a strong wind would break him in two. He grabbed the boy by the shoulder and held his eyes. "Sit next to me. If we overturn, hold onto me — my belt, my shirt, whatever you can grab. I'll get you ashore. What's your name."

"Tommy."

They pulled away from the ship, the crew manning the oars. George Lawrence sat in the prow, directing them, appearing to understand the way the ocean moved. For an hour they stayed in place, the crew red-faced and cursing. Then, suddenly, they reached the dip at the edge of the breakers and were forced to reverse to avoid overturning.

Lawrence yelled to the rowers. "Watch for a smooth. It's best to go in through one of those. I'll let you know when I see one."

The lifeboat swung around, leaving Frank and the boy facing the ship. He clung to the side, the boy holding his arm, and watched as the *Tararua* was pounded by heavy waves sweeping around the reef from the south. The captain had moved to the fore deck with a group of women and children; men had climbed the rigging, looking like flies on a monstrous web, waiting for a spider.

On the aft deck, which was higher above the water than the fore deck, a couple appeared, pushing against the wind. He watched, horrified, as they climbed up on the rail, kissed each, held hands, and leapt into the water. He couldn't be certain from this distance, but he thought it was the purser. Good swimmers might pull off a swim to safety after jumping fifteen feet onto brick-hard water, but this looked like a deliberate suicide.

Mette and Sarah Jane intruded into his thoughts, but he pushed them away. He was going to survive, for their sake, but he needed to concentrate.

He put one arm around Tommy and held on to him. The boy reminded him of his own adopted son, Joey; small, thin, eager to please, and hopeless when there was trouble.

"If you feel the boat tipping, grab my belt and don't let go."

He turned from the boy in time to see a dark shape slide by. He couldn't tell what it was: dolphin, seal, sea lion, a shark, possibly. But something large and ominous.

"Are there sharks in these waters?" he asked Lawrence.

"Great whites, for the most part. But they won't bother you unless you're bleeding. They go for blood. Although sometimes they mistake anyone in dark clothes for a seal. But they head for warmer waters when it gets this cold." He leaned over the gunnel and stared down into the water. "Did you see something?"

Frank was wearing a light blue shirt and buff-coloured trousers, but it didn't make him any more confident he wouldn't be attacked. "I thought I saw a shark. But I can't be sure."

"This is the time they feed," said one of the sailors. He had passed his oar to another crew member and was rubbing his hands to warm them, sweating heavily in the cold, damp air. "At dawn or in the evening. But they aren't often around these parts at this time of year. Now Sydney Harbour's a different kettle of fish. I once saw a shark take off a man's leg in a single bite, like it was a carrot..."

He stopped, clutching on the the side of the boat as it rose up on one end and thumped back down. "Whoa...what was that? Hold tight. Here we go."

"Make for the smooth," yelled Lawrence as the boat tilted over.

As he fell, Frank grabbed the brass polisher's hand. "Stay with me."

He was still holding the boy's hand as he surfaced five yards from the upturned boat, but something felt wrong. The boy was close, looking at Frank with wide eyes, his face pale.

Frank pulled him closer. "Are you alright?"

He shook his head. "Something bit me."

Frank kicked off his boots and raised the boy to the surface of the icy water. He could see a bite mark on his thigh, with blood starting to ooze from it.

"Christ...listen, I'm going to get you on shore and find a doctor. Hang on."

He lay on his back, the boy on top of him, and kicked hard. He couldn't see the smooth between the breakers this way, but he could move faster and had a better chance of making it to the beach.

In a fountain of water, a massive greyish brown shape rose from the water and splashed down in front of him. He jerked Tommy away from the beast, but it came at them, jaws open. Tucking the boy under one arm, he hit the shark's nose with all his strength. Dead eyes stared at him as he worked to scare it away, hitting it again and again. Finally, the shark slid back below the surface. Frank flipped on his back again and strained to kick as hard as he could. He was dammed if he was going to let this boy die.

But the shark had a different idea. He came up from below and thrust against Frank's back. He turned over and pounded at the nose again, looking into the emotionless eyes. "Leave him alone you bastard."

The shark dived again, and this time did not come up. The boy had closed his eyes now; his teeth were chattering, and his whole body was convulsed with the shakes.

Frank resumed his kicking. He couldn't see where he was in the ocean. He could be swimming out to sea for all he knew. But, unexpectedly, a gap opened between the breakers and they slipped through: George Lawrence's smooth. He kept on his back and was flung through the gap in the waves, both arms wrapped around the boy's narrow chest.

He felt rocks beneath his feet and pushed himself upright, only to be pulled back down by the undertow. As he struggled to his feet again, the boy slipped from his grasp.

He stood there, braced against the undertow, feeling the sand and stones melt beneath his feet, looking desperately for the brass polisher. The breakers came at him relentlessly, trying to throw him down and drag him out to sea. But he saw nothing.

COME TO GRIEF

"Sergeant Hardy, Sergeant Hardy. Give me your hand."

George Lawrence had steadied himself in the surf and was holding out his hand to Frank. He took it, and together they made it to the beach. Young Tommy was gone. He wanted to dive in and look for the boy, but had little strength remaining. It would be futile.

He crouched in the shallow water, exhausted and beaten.

George Lawrence had energy to burn, jumping up and down, ready to take off again.

"I was up on the rise," he said. "And I saw a building about half a mile away. I think there are men there. I'm going to find someone who can get to the nearest telegraph station and send for help. Will you come with me?"

Frank shook his head. He barely had enough strength left to stand. "I'll stay here and look for the boy."

George Lawrence gave him an odd look. "Are you sure you'll be alright? I'll come back and bring help. You rest for a bit. Don't risk your life in the surf."

Frank thanked him and watched as he ran towards the rise. It was too late for help. The boy must have drowned, if the shark hadn't got him. Feeling like it was his own son who'd been lost, he paced back and forth, staring at the water, hoping for some small sign of life, but seeing nothing.

6

The Tararua Comes to Grief

She'd hoped never to see him again, but there he was, waiting for the train to Bluff, standing on the edge of the platform staring down the track, watching for the train to arrive: the red-haired American, holding his brown leather Gladstone bag that looked like the one Mette carried, the one that had caused all the trouble yesterday and which now weighed a ton. She was overwhelmed by a desire to shove him onto the track, but instead, sat on a bench near the door to the ticket office and occupied herself with Sarah Jane.

She had dragged the Gladstone bag down from Mrs. Bentley's place, with her small bag over her shoulder and Sarah Jane tied securely on her back, and her arm was cramping from the weight.

The bag weighed a ton because she had collected Professor Mann's bloody manuscript last night, and it was the biggest pile of paper she'd ever seen, covered with tiny handwriting that looked like spiders had crawled across the page after stepping on an ink pad. To make matters worse, she had taken the abstract to read in bed and had fallen asleep after two pages.

51

So dull! It was all about the ancient Greeks and Romans, and how myths from every country were exactly the same. She knew that. Anyone did. She had been amused to hear some of Frank's scary childhood stories, and to discover how similar they were to stories her mother had frightened her with when she was a child in Denmark. Did someone really need to take a thousand pages to say that?

She had gone to Frau Mann's house the previous night, expecting to see a friendly woman with pink cheeks, soft grey hair and a full bosom, somewhat like her own mother. Instead, the door was opened by a thin-lipped woman with black hair pulled back into a tight bun, which lifted her eyebrows into an unnaturally surprised expression; she looked at Mette like she'd come to steal her chickens.

When Mette told Frau Mann she had come for the manuscript, Frau Mann glared at her and disappeared inside, leaving the door ajar. Mette stood there feeling foolish until Frau Mann returned carrying an old flour sack. She thrust it at Mette. "What a load of nonsense. I'm glad someone actually wants it." Then she slammed the door.

The young salesman took the flour sack and carried it back to the boarding house for her; she returned to her room, where Sarah Jane was sleeping, held in place by the two bags and a pillow. Mette was disappointed. She had imagined Frau Mann would ask her in for a cup of tea, and regale her with amusing stories about the professor.

When the train arrived, the conductor, an older man with a shock of white hair who reminded her of Father Christmas, helped her on board and found her a seat by the window. She cuddled Sarah Jane on her lap and leaned back, closing her eyes.

The conductor took her bag. "I'll put your bag in the luggage compartment by the exit, my dear. Then you can forget about it until we arrive in Invercargill."

She opened her eyes, shading them against the sun. "When will that be?"

He inspected his watch. "We arrive in Invercargill at five o'clock. After half an hour, we continue on to Bluff to arrive at half past five. Will someone be meeting you?"

"My husband. He's on the *Tararua*. It's due to dock at noon."

"Excellent. You're going to have a long day, my dear. I hope you brought some food with you. You'll be able to buy refreshments at Balclutha and Wyndham, but as I said, I'll bring you a cup of tea once we're on the way."

She'd always been a little afraid of trains, fearful that they would come off the track, trapping her inside like a coffin, or that someone would open a window and she — or, these days, Sarah Jane — would be sucked out. But she was tired, and happy to be settled in one place for a few hours. The American was not in her carriage, thank heavens. She thought she saw him getting on the next one. If he'd been there, sitting close to her, it would have ruined her trip. Now she could look out at the beautiful scenery and enjoy herself. She looked forward to the conductor's cup of tea. She hadn't had time for breakfast as she had to spend time in her room feeding and dressing Sarah Jane, but Mrs. Bentley had given her a Scotch scone with a wedge of butter inside, which would be perfect with tea.

The driver sounded the whistle, and a blast of hot steam billowed out the side of the engine. She watched the platform, expecting it to disappear slowly from view, but a tall, thin man in a dark navy suit had arrived and was speaking to the station master. The station master had the flag in one hand, ready to signal departure to the engineer, but he stopped while he listened to the man. After a few minutes he pointed to her carriage; was he pointing at her? Of course he was not. Why would he point at her? The carriage was at least half full.

The train began to move, the pistons thumping. She felt the vibrations all through her body, and held on to the seat to make sure she didn't fall off. The man in the navy suit seemed to decide something. He turned and sprinted towards the train, jumped at the door, hung for a while on the step, and then pulled himself into the carriage. He took a seat not far from Mette and looked at his watch before glancing around. She caught his eye and looked away. He looked pleased with himself.

She had met many policemen in the last three years, and thought she recognized one when she saw one. She was sure this man must be an inspector, and he was following someone. She hoped very much that he was following the American with red hair and whiskers, who had criminal written all over him, in her opinion.

The day dragged on and the never-ending sounds and movement of the train lulled her into a half sleep. They stopped at Balclutha for refreshments, and Mette decided to buy herself more tea and a sandwich from the refreshment stand at the end of the platform. She left Sarah Jane with a large, comfortable Maori woman who had been smiling at her in a friendly way, jumped off the train, and hurried to the refreshment stand, nervous the whole time that the train would leave without her, taking Sarah Jane off to who knew where.

As she ordered her sandwich — thinly-sliced tongue, her favourite — the man she suspected was a policeman appeared beside her and asked for a Scotch egg and a bottle of ginger ale.

He nodded at Mette, his face gloomy. She noticed a drip of something hanging off the end of his nose, and had to force herself not to wipe it away with her handkerchief. She nodded back, not speaking.

"About time we stopped for refreshments, isn't it?" he asked suddenly.

She smiled at him, wondering why he was speaking to her. Men seldom spoke to women who were alone.

"Where are you off to?"

She thought it was none of his business, but told him anyway. He was a nondescript fellow, with his navy suit, dark brown hair parted on one side and combed flat across his forehead. His skin was pale, as if he spent all his time indoors, bloodless, almost. The kind of man who would blend into a crowd, which, she supposed, was his job, really. The constabulary had come a long way from the days when they dressed in blanket kilts and galloped through the bush in groups, carbines resting on saddles, ready to shoot at anything that moved. He looked more like a bank teller or a law clerk, but the way he constantly checked his surroundings confirmed for her the suspicion that he was a policeman.

There was no sign of the red-haired American on the platform, although she thought she saw him in the carriage next to hers, his hand resting on the sill of the open window, puffing cigarette smoke. She was glad she'd persuaded Frank to give up smoking. He'd stopped drinking as well, more or less, but decided an occasional glass of beer wouldn't hurt him.

He claimed the beer relaxed him, which she knew meant it stopped him worrying about everything.

When she returned to the carriage, Sarah Jane had fallen asleep on the Maori woman's comfortable breasts, so Mette sat beside her and left the baby where she was. She had purchased a slice of tea cake for the woman, who took it without disturbing Sarah Jane.

"*Ataahua.*" She smiled down at Sarah Jane, whose face was pressed against her breast, her lips working as she dreamed about feeding. Mette understood a few Maori words, but not that one. She assumed it was something pleasant and smiled back. She'd discovered over the years that a smile got you a long way.

The sandwich and tea, and the soft arm of the Maori woman, soon put Mette to sleep as well.

She awoke when the woman shook her arm. "*Mahue,*" she said. "Wyndham."

She was obviously getting off at Wyndham.

She took Sarah Jane and followed the Maori woman to the exit, hoping to get a breath of fresh air while the train was at the station. The departing passengers were milling around, finding their bags, and greeting friends and family. The engineer had climbed from the engine and was inspecting something on the side.

A man came out of the waiting room and yelled to the engineer, who called back, "Any casualties?"

For a minute she could not believe what she was hearing.

"What did he say?" she asked the policeman, who was standing behind her in the aisle.

"Something about the *Tararua,*" he said. "The steamer. I

think he said it's come to grief."

"Come to…what does that mean?"

"Sunk, I think. Off Fortrose."

She stared at him in horror. "Sunk? The *Tararua*? That's not possible; Frank…I have to get off the train…"

She pushed past him back to her seat and picked up her small bag from the floor where she had left it. She returned to the baggage room near the exit and looked for her Gladstone bag. Of course there were two bags that looked the same, which made her angry again, but the first one she picked up was heavy, so she knew it was hers. Loaded down with the two bags and Sarah Jane, she hurried to the exit again.

The man in the navy suit was waiting for her at the bottom of the steps. "Here, pass me your bag and I'll help you down."

She obeyed numbly.

"Please, how can I find out more about the ship…the *Tararua*. I need…my husband is…"

She was unable to continue. Her throat had closed up with terror and her neck was aching.

Taking her arm, he escorted her over to the station master's office. She couldn't believe how calm he was. "This lady needs to know about the *Tararua*. Her husband is on board."

The station master patted her on the shoulder. "Nothing to worry about, my dear. The ship ran aground on a reef near Toi Toi Bay early this morning. Everyone's safe. A sailor swam ashore and someone brought him here to the telegraph station. The morning operator sent off a telegram to Bluff and I just heard that the *Hawea* has gone to help. The *Kaikanui* is on its way as well and will take all the passengers back to Dunedin."

Relief flooded over her, but she was not completely reassured.

"Are you sure no one was hurt?"

"The telegraph office is across the road. You could ask the operator if he's heard anything more."

She left her bag on the station and hurried over to the telegraph office, the policeman still with her. She was grateful, now, that he was here, and seemed to have forgotten about the person he'd been following. She didn't think she could cope with this alone.

The telegraph operator was listening to a chattering machine, writing down a message that had just come in. Before she could ask him anything, he turned, his face pale.

"Fearful loss of life. Over one hundred drowned. It's the worst disaster the country has ever seen."

Mette heard no more. She felt the policeman catch her and Sarah Jane as her legs gave way, and everything faded to darkness.

7

Night Fires

The first body came ashore soon after George Lawrence disappeared over the rise on his way to the hut where he'd seen men. To keep himself warm, but also because he was desperate to find someone, anyone, from the lifeboat, Frank had increased his range, pacing along the stony beach from one end to the other — almost a mile, he estimated — clambering up the rocks that ran up to the beach from the reef at the southern end, scanning the reef for signs of life other than fur seals, gannets and gulls, and then walking to the other end, scouring the shoreline, until he reached the cliffs that blocked him from going further now the tide was in.

He had lost his boots in the water, and was forced to weave his way between the stones and driftwood in his stockinged feet above the high tide mark where the sand was firmer. Half way along he spotted a log being buffeted by the surf. Thinking it was part of the lifeboat, he waded in to check before the undertow dragged it back out to sea; it was one of the crewmen from the lifeboat, his trousers ripped off in the ocean, wearing nothing but his shirt. He dragged the body above the high tide mark and lay it face down on the stones. The time for burial would come later, when the bodies had been identified.

Before George Lawrence returned, Frank had found three more bodies. One man surfaced between the line of waves, his arms flailing in panic, unable to get himself to the shallow water. Frank waded out as far as he could and yelled to the man to get himself inside the line of breakers. The man had made headway and was within reach when the undertow carried him back out. Frank waited until he came in a second time, looking weaker. This time he said nothing. He looked at Frank, who was up to his chest in the water holding himself steady, and gave in.

Two more men managed to make it ashore: William Hill, a steerage passenger, and the ship's head cook, Antonio Micalef. After a short discussion the two went to look for farms nearby. Frank remained on the beach, hoping the boy would, against all odds, come ashore alive.

He was at the reef end of the beach when George Lawrence returned. They walked along the shore together.

"You got help?"

"I was lucky. That hut I saw in the distance was the out-station of a run holding and there were men inside having breakfast. I asked where the nearest telegraph station was, and they told me thirty or forty miles away, in Wyndham."

The sea washed over their feet and retreated, leaving a child's shoe. Lawrence picked it up and stared at it blankly. "One of the men offered to ride to the telegraph station. He asked me if anyone had drowned, and I said 'I'm not sure, but I'm the first ashore.' Has anyone drowned, Sergeant?"

"I'm afraid so," said Frank. "I've found three bodies. I don't think any of the crew on our lifeboat survived. They'd be in by now. But two men swam in from the lifeboat that overturned on the reef. They've gone to get help from local settlers."

"Terrible." Lawrence tossed the child's shoe away. "It's just terrible. I can't believe I'm alive. Why me?"

"What did you tell them to say in the telegram? And where did you send it?"

"To the Union Steam Ship Company in Dunedin. I told them to say the *Tararua* is on the Otara Reef and to please send help immediately."

"Dunedin," said Frank. That would mean several hours before help would arrive, although the shipping office in Dunedin would probably telegraph Bluff. He wondered how far it was to Bluff Harbour from the Otara Reef. No more than twenty miles. It might have been better for the lifeboat to get out past the breakers and head south to Bluff Harbour. With eight men taking turns at the oars, the boat would go that far in seven or eight hours. Bounty Bligh had made it all the way to Timor after his crew set him adrift, almost four thousand miles.

Eventually, settlers from nearby farms began to stream down through the sand hills with food, blankets and matches. A lifeboat had washed ashore with a large hole in the side, and men with tools and tried to repair it. Someone started a fire on the beach, so that anyone coming from the ship in the dark would have a place to aim for now that night had returned. One of the women gave him a slab of mutton on bread, and a mug of beer, and he realized it was the first time he'd eaten all day.

"Did you have anyone on the ship?" she asked, as she handed him the food. She was a woman of about sixty with a deeply lined face and steel grey hair, who looked like she'd spent years running a farm kitchen, feeding shearers, making clothes for the family, and bringing up children to be good citizens. The best kind of New Zealand woman. She might not make a show of sympathy, but everything she did would be for the purpose of improving the lives of others.

"I was travelling alone." He bit into the bread and mutton and took a swig of beer. "My wife and daughter were with me, but they disembarked in Dunedin. She's supposed to be meeting me in Bluff."

"In that case you should go to Bluff," she said firmly. "Otherwise, when she gets there she'll hear about the ship sinking and she'll be worried."

That was something he hadn't thought of. "I'll go as soon as it gets light. What's the best way to get there?"

"Walk along the coast to Fortrose. It's about ten miles away. From there you can take the daily coach. Or get a horse if you can find one. I don't think there's a livery stable in Fortrose, but someone will let you borrow a horse, I'm sure, given what's happened. If you have any problems, come back here and ask for Otara Station or Brunton's place. We'll fix you up with something."

Frank huddled by the fire with the settlers, who were chatting quietly. He fell asleep with his head cradled on his knees, but was awoken by the distant sound of screams and voices.

He raised his head. He felt groggy, and his muscles ached from the effort he'd made swimming ashore from the lifeboat. "What's going on?"

Groups of women were clustered at the waterline, crying and holding each other.

"The ship split in half and it's sinking. We can hear them screaming out there, but we can't help them."

The screams sounded eerily close, as the passengers of the Tararua begged for help. He felt useless. Even if he could swim out to the ship, he wouldn't be able to swim back with anyone. He thought of Mette and Sarah Jane again, thankful that they weren't on the ship, and that he had not run after them in Port Chalmers and forced them to return. What would he do now if they were still out there? He had no doubt about that. He would swim out and do everything he could to save them, even if he died trying.

He climbed up the rocks, thinking he might be able to make his way out on the reef and get as near as he could to the ship, and then swim the rest of the way. It was low tide and the reef was above water. But as he peered into the darkness, the broken hull of the *Tararua* slipped out of sight and the screaming stopped.

A few more people came ashore, mainly men from steerage who were used to hard physical work and were strong swimmers. He paced up and down the beach looking for anyone who might need help.

He had almost given up, when he saw a flash of light. It looked like a mirror, reflecting off a dark shape on the surface.

He waded in as far as he could, bracing himself again the pull of the undertow.

"Is someone there?"

Above the noise of the ocean he heard the cry of a child, a baby. He knew the sound; he had awoken to it many times.

"Someone's out there," said a voice behind him.

The cook waded out beside him. "I just pulled a man ashore down the beach. He was alive."

Frank shaded his eyes. He was sure he could see something. What was it? "How did you get ashore? Were you in a lifeboat?"

The cook shook his head. "I swam. I'm from Malta. I've lived by the sea my whole life, on boats, fishing for bream, mullet, sardines...no sharks though. I saw a shark as I came in. A big one. Maybe that's a shark you can see."

"No. I I heard a baby crying," said Frank. "And I saw a flash of light. If I swim out to look for it, will you stay on the shore to help me in?"

The cook nodded. "I'll be here. Up on the sandhill where I can see the water. I'll come down when I see you coming."

Frank waited, listening, until he heard the cry again. He returned to the beach and dropped his shirt on the sand. Then he waded out up to his waist and dived into the next wave as it crested, staying low as long as he could and pulling himself through the water. He came up on the far side in time to see another wave bearing down on him. He took two deep breaths and went under the second wave. The water was calmer beneath the waves, and the undertow was no longer a factor. He swam for as long as he could hold his breath.

This time he surfaced out beyond the breakers. The sea was calm, the waves just starting to form, and he trod water, listening for the sound of the baby.

When it came, it was close, but weak. He tried to push himself up and out of the water, circling, looking for it. Suddenly it was next to him: a wooden gate, bobbing in the sea. A woman lay across the gate on her side, the baby held tightly in her crossed arms, her eyes closed.

He shook her arm to let her know he was there, but her eyes remained closed. She was wearing a silver bracelet — the shiny thing in the water that he had seen from the shore. His limbs were starting to seize up with the cold, and he knew he should start heading back to shore.

He shook her arm again, and then edged up onto the gate and tried to pry open her eye. Frozen shut. She was dead, but the child was not.

The gate dipped under the water, covering the woman's arm and lapping at the baby. He slipped off and it bounced back up to the surface. The baby was looking at him through rime-covered eyes, held tight in its mother's immovable arms, but alive. He turned the gate towards the beach and started kicking. If he could catch a wave at the right moment, he could ride in on it. With luck, that would take him to the beach where the cook would be waiting to help them ashore.

He was lined up, ready to float in with the next wave, when something grabbed him by the ankle. Holding the gate with one hand, he turned, ready to kick the shark on the nose, and found William Sampson floundering in the water behind him.

"Help me, help me."

"I can't…you're almost to the shore. Keep…" He took in a mouthful of water, and stopped, coughing. "Swim in with a wave. There's a man on shore who'll help you to land."

Sampson slipped beneath the water and surfaced, gagging and flailing.

"Can't swim any longer." His voice was raspy and he sounded exhausted. "Give me the gate."

Frank gave the gate a push away from Sampson, but it spun back towards him. He grabbed it by one edge and attempted to pull himself onto it, tilting it almost vertical.

"Help me up, you have to help me up."

Frank tugged the gate away from him. "You'll pull it under and kill the baby."

65

"Who cares? The mother's dead. Push them both off and let me on."

Frank could see a likely looking wave coming. He raised his knees to his chest and kicked hard, shoving Sampson away. "The mother's dead but the baby isn't, and I can't pry it from its mother's arms out here. I'm going to take the whole thing ashore and pull them apart."

The wave was almost upon him. He held the gate with both hands and kicked as hard as he could.

"Don't leave me." Sampson coughed. "Listen, I know who you are. I know what you want. I can help you."

Frank ignored him and kept going. The wave was almost on them.

"I can tell you about the gold…I know where it is…but you have to give me the gate."

The wave lifted Frank's body, and with it the gate and its burden.

As he gained speed on the crest, he looked back and yelled to Sampson. "Find your own way in. I'm not letting another child die."

Then he was flying forward, clutching the gate, looking into the unresponsive eyes of the dead mother with the child in her arms.

The Maltese cook was waiting for him on the beach. He ran into the surf and dragged in the gate with its two occupants. "I almost gave up on you," said the cook. "I thought you weren't coming back. Give me a hand and we'll take this up higher."

Once the gate with the mother and child were past the high water mark, Frank collapsed on his knees, vomiting sea water. The cook knelt by the gate and pulled open the mother's arms, removing the child.

"This woman is dead. Did you know that?"

Frank nodded. He was unbelievably weary.

"You better take this baby to the fire. Warm her up."

"It's a girl?"

The cook opened the baby's clothing and peered inside. "I think so." He handed the baby to Frank. She was shivering, but silent, looking at him closely like her life depended on him.

"What am I going to do with her? Once she's warmed up, I mean."

The Maltese cook shrugged. "I don't know about babies," he said. "Talk to the women. Maybe one of them can take her."

"She looks to be about the same age as my daughter." Frank's body was warming up. He picked up his shirt and shrugged one arm on at a time, still holding the child. Then he buttoned it up with the baby inside, in the way he often carried Sarah Jane. She rubbed her nose against his chest and whimpered.

"Nothing there, sorry." He dried her hair with his sleeve and turned to the cook. "Thank you for helping me in, Mr...what did you say your name was?"

"Antonio." He reached out and patted the baby's head, smiling down at her. "Antonio Miscalef. Pleased to meet you. And what's your name?"

"Hardy, Frank Hardy."

They walked to the fire together, not saying much. The baby had settled in against Frank and seemed happy, although she was sucking her thumb ferociously. Mette did not like Sarah Jane sucking her thumb, and pulled it out if she started. But watching the child, he could only think that she found it comforting. And she needed some comfort now.

William Hill was warming himself by the fire. He saw them

coming and ran down the beach to meet them.

"You found my baby?"

Frank opened his shirt to show the infant to Hill, deciding not to mention the mother just yet. "Is she yours?"

Hill touched the baby's head gently and began to cry.

"No, no, Eliza, no!"

Frank clasped William Hill by the shoulder. "She's alive, Mr. Hill, she's alive."

"But it's not her, it's not my…" Hill dropped to the ground in a dead faint. The cook kneeled by him and flicked him on the ear with one finger. "It's alright, Mr. Hill, we'll find your baby as well."

The woman from Otara Station was at the fire, feeding a man who had just come ashore. She nodded at Frank and continued to wield the spoon. "What have you found, Sergeant?"

"A baby," he said. "A little girl. Her mother's dead. I left her where she came ashore."

"Is the baby hungry?"

"She must be. I've been warming her up."

She reached into a bag at her feet and pulled out a tin and an opener. "Here's some condensed milk. Mix it with water and give her some in a cup." She rummaged in her bag again. "Here's a cup."

"Can she drink from a cup?"

She ran a finger over the baby's gums. "She has some teeth. I'd say she's close to a year old. By that age they can usually drink from a cup."

He opened the tin, poured the condensed milk into the cup, and topped it up with water. The baby drank it enthusiastically, slopping it down her cheeks. When she finished she started to whimper. He poured another cup.

"Mrs. Brunton, can you take this baby to your farm when you return there?"

Mrs. Brunton looked at him with an odd expression on her face. "All my people are already working full tilt," she said. "They're cooking for survivors, bringing food to the beach, finding clothing. And it's only going to get busier when the police and more searchers arrive. I can't spare anyone to care for a baby this young. I'm sorry."

"What am I going to do with her?"

"Isn't your wife waiting for you in Bluff. Take the baby there and give her to your wife until you can find a relative. Didn't you say you have a young baby yourself?"

He nodded. That seemed to solve two problems at once, although he wasn't sure what Mette would have to say about it. "I'll do that. I'll leave at first light. Is there anywhere I can get some sleep, and the baby as well?"

She finished spooning the soup and put the mug into her bag.

"I'm walking back to the farm now. Come with me. I'll find you a spot in the shearing shed, and a blanket. We've got a lot of people sleeping at our station already. Perhaps one of them is the baby's father."

He hadn't thought of the father. But when he did an image resurfaced in his mind: the young woman with the baby coming up the gangplank in Port Chalmers as he took Mette to the train. It was her: the woman floating on the gate was the same woman he had seen coming up the gangplank. And she'd had a young man with her, a young man with fair hair like hers. If he could find that man, his problems would be over, and he wouldn't have to ask Mette to care for the child.

8

Death on the Beach

A hiss of steam followed by a piercing train whistle penetrated Mette's consciousness. She sat up in a panic. "My baby — Sarah Jane. She's on the train. Don't let it leave."

"Don't worry, miss, she's here. I have her." The man in the navy suit squatted beside her, a squirming Sarah Jane propped awkwardly on his knee as if he'd never held a baby before. It reminded her of someone else she'd seen recently holding a baby the wrong way. Who was that? Her brain was too fuzzy to think about it.

Then she remembered where she was. "Frank?"

The three men surrounding her eyed each other, waiting for someone else to speak.

"What happened to my husband? He was on the ship that went down."

"I haven't received a list of fatal...of survivors yet," said the telegraph operator. "There's a lot of confusion. No one seems to know anything. Just that..."

She finished his sentence, her heart heavy. "...a hundred people drowned."

"Twenty survived," said the man in the navy suit. "If your husband can swim, he's probably one of them. All the survivors were men, most of them passengers."

"He's a very good swimmer." Mette pressed her hand against her mouth and tried not to sob as a memory rose in her mind: she and Frank were in the creek that ran beside their property up near Feilding, on a sweltering hot day last summer. They were soaking themselves in the cool waters of the creek, in the pool above the waterfall, when Frank swam from the far side and grabbed her by the foot, without surfacing to take a breath. She had laughed and accused him of showing off. He must be among the survivors.

"How can I find out?"

"I've had a few telegrams." The telegraph operator pointed to a pile of paper. "But it's been a different list of names each time. I don't remember seeing a Hardy on any of the lists. The best way know for certain would be to go there and search for him. "

She knew he meant search for his body, but brushed the thought aside. Frank was alive and she had to find him. "Go where?"

"Fortrose."

She was about to ask him how she could get to Fortrose, when he added, "There's a coach to Fortrose leaving within the hour. It's the last one today and it arrives in Fortrose at dusk. It's not a good coach for a lady, if you don't have anywhere to stay."

She took Sarah Jane from navy suit and struggled to her feet.

"I want to go there. To Fortrose."

"I'll come with you then," he said. "I'd like to understand what happened and to see if I can do anything; I'm sure you could do with the assistance."

"Weren't you on your way somewhere?"

"At times like this, everything stops, and one has to do what's necessary."

Before she had a chance to be more worried about Frank, she was in the coach with the man in the navy suit. He'd sent a telegram to someone in Dunedin telling them where he was going, and had climbed in to the seat across from her, where she sat with Sarah Jane on her knee, her bags by her feet.

He settled into the centre of the seat, sitting upright, his hands laid neatly along his knees. She noticed he still had a drip on the end of his nose. Instead of wanting to wipe it off, now she wanted to throw a handkerchief at him.

He stared at her, his eyes expressionless. "This won't last long."

"What won't last long?" Nothing was making sense to her at the moment.

"No other passengers. By tomorrow the whole world will be heading for Fortrose. Friends and relatives, newspapermen, government officials, men from the shipping company, police..."

Mette was trying to ignore the dreadful image of Frank's body sprawled on the beach, so she blurted out the first thing that came into her mind

"You're a policeman, aren't you?"

He stared at her, then said quietly, "What makes you think that?"

"I've known a lot of policemen. And you look like one."

She realized she had allowed him to help her because she assumed he was a policeman. But what if she was wrong?

Frank would be annoyed if…but she couldn't think about Frank. He *was* alive. She refused to imagine her life without him.

"Well, are you a police constable?"

"Not exactly."

"A private investigator?"

"You know about private investigators as well, do you?"

She looked at him closely for the first time. He was young — not much older than she was. Probably twenty-seven or twenty-eight, with a thin face and that long, drippy nose. He had the kind of face you might not remember and would find hard to describe. Not a constable, she decided. Perhaps someone who worked for a private investigator and followed people for a living. "My husband was once a private investigator."

"Was he indeed?" He smiled knowingly.

Sarah Jane had been behaving herself since they got off the train. But things had gone too far, and she pulled at Mette's buttons, whining, and wanting to feed. They wouldn't arrive in Fortrose for another hour and a half, and Sarah Jane wasn't going to wait that long.

"I'm sorry Mr….what did you say your name was? I need to feed and change my little one. You can ride up the front with the driver for a while if you wish."

"Smith," he said. "Roderick Smith. Go ahead. I've seen women feeding babies before."

He watched her closely as she unbuttoned her dress and put Sarah Jane to her breast, seeming surprised when the baby latched on. Had he not expected Sarah Jane to find anything?

"Is it difficult feeding a baby who isn't yours?" he asked as she was moving Sarah Jane from one side to the other.

For a minute she couldn't believe what she'd heard. "Not mine? Of course Sarah Jane is mine." Her beautiful baby was so much like Frank; she wanted to cry.

"She doesn't resemble you at all. You're so fair, and she's dark-eyed and olive skinned. I didn't think that was possible."

Mette didn't answer, but stared out the window as they bumped through the approaching twilight along the rutted, un-metalled road towards Fortrose. She felt like she was in limbo. Where was Frank, and was he still alive?

They arrived in Fortrose to find a small town in chaos. Dozens of people had arrived already, and a coach was sitting outside a ramshackle hotel while the driver argued with the hotel keeper, standing on his verandah with a coach light in his hand and a blanket over his shoulders. No room at the inn, apparently, not tonight, even for a member of parliament. She didn't care where she spent the night. She could sleep under a bridge if necessary. She carried Sarah Jane down the steps, and watched as the coachman unloaded her bags.

"Where should I take these?" he asked. "Have you booked a room at a hotel? There's nothing available, you know."

"I don't know what to do." She was hungry and exhausted. "I need to get out to the shipwreck. I don't want to spend the night in Fortrose. I want to keep going. I have to."

"Hmmm. You can't go out there now. It's getting dark," he said. "You'll fall off a cliff."

"Where can I stay then?"

Mr. Smith had come around the coach and was standing behind her, his hands hanging by his side. She wished he would go away. The coachman looked from one to another, and she realized he thought they were husband and wife.

"Why don't you sleep in my coach? I'm not leaving until mid morning tomorrow. I have a room with a lady friend. I'll leave the coach down near the jetty overnight. When you're ready, just slide in and find yourself a place to sleep."

Mr. Smith thanked the driver. She was annoyed. Now she would be spending the night in the coach with this man; she wanted to be alone with Sarah Jane so she could cry herself to sleep.

A dusty, pot-holed road ran beside the ocean, with a few wagons and horses still at work. At one end of the road, a wooden jetty pushed out into the water, with small ships and fishing boats moored on either side. Two more ships sat at anchor in the bay. Above the harbour to the east, a pale sliver of moon was surrounded by cloud that reflected the pink and orange of the setting sun to the west.

She left her bags in the coach and walked along the harbour, trying to calm herself. She heard Mr. Smith behind her, which made her walk faster. If only she could get away from him. Her fear for Frank had turned to anger, and she wanted nothing more than to hit someone. If he didn't go away soon, she would slap him.

On the jetty, people milled around the goods shed, watching two men carrying a body from a small ship docked at the jetty. Anxious to find out what they were carrying, she ran towards the goods shed clutching Sarah Jane in her arms, pushing past crowds of men.

She reached the shed as the body arrived at the shed; one man held the body — the long body — under the knees, another under the arms. Her throat tightened again.

"Who is it?" She scrabbled at the corner of the tarpaulin with her free hand, trying to pull it away from the face. She was sure it was Frank.

"It's the captain." The man carrying the body by the shoulders pulled it away from her. "Captain Garrard. We found him at the far end of the beach on the other side of the point, north of where the boat went down. His body was brought in by the high tide and left there. His legs were tangled up in kelp, which would have hampered his efforts to save himself."

"Lying in the shallows, his arms stretched out like he was still swimming," said the man holding the lower end of the body. They carried the captain's body into the shed, and Mette and Smith followed them as they laid it on the floor at the end a row of other shrouded bodies. She could not see anyone else tall in the row, but there were several very small shapes; she hugged Sarah Jane and turned away. It was unimaginable.

"Poor sod would have made it, if not for the kelp." The first man shook his head sadly.

"I heard he was a first class swimmer," said the second man. "And he'd been shipwrecked before, so they say, on an island in the Bay of Fundy in the middle of winter. He made his way up an icy cliff and through the snowdrifts to a fisherman's cottage and saved…"

Although she was not used to being rude to men, Mette could stand it no longer. "Please…I'm trying to find my husband. He was on the ship."

"Name?"

"Hardy. Sergeant Frank Hardy."

The men exchanged glances and shrugged.

"Haven't heard that name. What does he look like?"

"Tall, dark eyes and hair…"

"They found the body of a tall dark man on the beach near the wreck," said one. "Came in holding on to a plank. The settlers tried to pull him in but couldn't. The sea kept taking him back out. When they finally got him in, it was too late. He died on the beach without telling them his name."

Mette turned to Mr. Smith, who had followed her and was watching her closely. He suddenly seemed more necessary. Her throat was tightening again, and she found it hard to speak above a whisper.

"I have to go there, to the beach. Tonight. I can't wait until morning. Will you come with me?"

"It's a good ten-mile walk, miss," said one of the men. "And terrible in the dark. You'd be walking along a stony beach most of the time, although the lagoon on this side of the point is smooth when the tide's out. I think they might have taken that particular body to Otara Station. Mr. Brunton comes in to town every day with his wagon, bringing in food for the workers. The next time he comes in you could ask him if he's seen the…your husband, or you could go with him to look for yourself."

A third man had come through the door, and interjected. "Mr. Brunton is bringing in coffins now. We're burying the bodies out near the point, in a special graveyard. They're calling it Tararua Acre. I'm getting a team together to dig the graves."

That was worse. She might walk all the way to the beach near the wreck and find nothing but unmarked graves. She might never know what happened to him.

"Is there someone who could take us out there in a wagon, first thing in the morning?" asked Smith.

"I'll be loading the bodies tonight and taking them out tomorrow at sunrise," said the man. "Help me get a few of these bodies on the wagon and I'll take you with me. There won't be much room, but enough for the two of you. Who did you lose?"

"My husband." Mette could hardly bear to say those words. "At least, I hope he isn't lost. But I need to be sure."

The man nodded. "I understand. The shipping office will have a list of who died in due course. But you'll want to know as soon as you can."

"Does anyone have a list of passengers?" asked Smith.

The man pulled a crumpled piece of paper from his pocket. "I got this passenger manifest from the shipping office in the Bluff. When I hear about a body or someone being saved I make a mark beside the name on the list."

Smith scanned the manifest and looked sideways at Mette. "There's no Hardy here. Was he travelling under a false name?"

She took the manifest from him. He was right. Frank's name was not there. She returned it, puzzled. "But he *was* on the ship. We both were. I disembarked in Port Chalmers and went into Dunedin for the night, because I had a manuscript to pick up. I stayed with Mrs. Bentley on Moray Place. Then I took the train…I was on my way to Bluff…"

He looked at the list again. "Are you sure he didn't disembark in Dunedin as well? This manifest is for passengers who were still on board when the ship left Dunedin."

"He took me to the train and went back to the ship."

"You saw him boarding? Actually on the gang plank?"

Now that she thought about it, she hadn't seen him after he left her. Perhaps he'd followed someone. But she didn't want to say that to Mr. Smith, who did not seem to believe that Frank even existed. "He went back on board. He had something important he had to do."

After an uncomfortable night in the coach, pretending she was alone and not sleeping at all, Mette was up as soon as she caught the faintest pink streak in the eastern sky. Mr. Smith, who had sat with his arms crossed in the corner of the coach, snoring, woke up as soon as she moved. "Best get to that wagon." He yawned. "You stay here and I'll help load the bodies."

The wagon left Fortrose as soon as the sun broke above the horizon, with Mette and Mr. Smith squashed up on the front seat with the driver. Behind them, five bodies were piled up like logs. She tried to keep her eyes on the road in front of them, concentrating on Sarah Jane, but could not avoid the smell emanating from the back of the wagon. She had her small bag with her, and had left the heavy one at the post office, saying she would send for it when she could. The ridiculous manuscript had made things more difficult for her.

As they left town, they passed another wagon entering Fortrose.

The driver raised his whip in salute. "There's Mr. Brunton, bringing in coffins. And some more searchers, I hope."

Mette had been hugging Sarah Jane, resting her head on the baby's head for comfort, finally letting the tears flow. She glanced up. The wagon had moved past them quickly, but for a wonderful minute she thought she saw Frank. The man was facing away from her. She stared back as the wagon receded. It could be Frank, but she was overcome with the knowledge that she would see him everywhere, for the rest of her life. The man had his head down, gazing at a child he held in his arms.

79

Not Frank then, but a grieving father who had lost some of his family, coming to Fortrose to search for a survivor or a body, as she herself had done.

An hour later, they arrived at the new graveyard near the site of the wreck. Ominous cliffs rose in the distance, shrouded by low-lying clouds, and a cold wind was coming in off the ocean. Closer, the cliffs turned into sand hills fronted by a beach covered in debris from the shipwreck. Teams of men were working in a grassy paddock, digging one grave after another to accommodate the neat rows of bodies nearby.

While the driver and Mr. Smith carried the bodies from the wagon and laid them with the others, Mette went along the row of bodies and looked for Frank. Only one was tall enough to be him, and she tugged back the tarpaulin. A tall, dark-haired man, but not Frank.

"That one came ashore yesterday," said one of the diggers. "He was alive and holding on to a board, and the settlers tried to help him. He died on the beach after they got him in."

"Have you seen another tall, dark man?"

The grave digger shook his head. "Not me, no. But there are people on the beach who've been here a lot of the time, like Mrs. Brunton from Otara Station. I saw her arrive a few minutes ago. Look for her by the fire."

Without stopping to tell Mr. Smith where she was going, Mette dragged herself and Sarah Jane over the sand hills to the beach. She could see a group of people gathered around the fire. A stream of searchers were coming and going, carrying things they'd found on the shore. As far as she could see, items from the ship littered the beach: doors, ladders, clothing and suitcases. One man held two mail bags, another a small wooden chest.

An older woman seemed to be in charge, directing the searchers and handing out food. Mette went up to her and asked abruptly, "I'm looking for my husband. Have you seen a tall, dark man…"

"Sergeant Hardy, you mean?"

Mette almost dropped Sarah Jane on the sand, but managed to catch her before she hit the ground. "You've seen him? His body?"

"Not his body, my dear." The woman smiled. "Sergeant Hardy himself. He spent last night at our station and went into Fortrose with my husband in the wagon this morning. I'm Mrs. Brunton."

Mette was overcome with joy. Frank was alive. Now all she had to do was get to him. She would go back to Fortrose and everything would return to normal.

She turned, wondering what had happened to Mr. Smith.

Mr. Smith was with an older man sporting a thin moustache, obviously a senior police officer. They walked over, Mr. Smith talking and gesturing, the other man frowning and nodding.

Mrs. Brunton stroked Sarah Jane's head. "He'll be pleased to see you both, my dear. He's been carrying the baby around, and he…"

"The baby?" asked Mette. "Whose baby?"

"Whose baby?" Mr. Smith repeated. "You see Tuohy? She doesn't even know whose baby it is."

No, no. You misunderstood. I didn't mean this baby. I meant the baby with my husband."

Mrs. Brunton stepped in to defend Mette. "I'm Mrs. Brunton from Otara Station," she said briskly. "And I don't have a clue whose baby it is, but her husband saved its life."

81

The man with Roderick Smith glanced at him and said in voice that sounded much too deferential for Mette, "What would you like me to do, sir?"

Smith stared at Mette for two minutes, one finger resting on his cheek, then made a decision. "Arrest her. She doesn't even know who the baby belongs to. I don't believe anything she says. We'll take her to Invercargill and sort it out there."

As Mette stared in horror at Mr. Smith, his companion uttered words Mette had heard before, but never in respect to her own self.

"Mrs. Hardy, I'm arresting you for the kidnapping of a female child in Dunedin on Wednesday, April the twenty-seventh. If you have anything to say in your own defence, please say it now."

9

Brunton's Station

Otara Station, where Mrs. Brunton took Frank, had become a centre of operations since the sinking of the Tararua. Women bustled around preparing food and packing it in boxes, which they left in a wheelbarrow at the door to the kitchen for Mrs. Brunton to take to the searchers and survivors. As they walked up from the beach he could see it was a large, prosperous sheep station. There were worse places he could find himself, after the horror of the wreck.

He still had his money belt with eight pounds he'd made from the current crop of horses, but he'd lost his boots, his jacket, and his bag — the new one he'd bought from Kirkcaldie and Stains with his profits from the previous trip. The bag had contained a change of under clothing and the supply of food he always carried him: hard tack, barley sugar and tins of sardines.

He'd replaced the bag with the burden of a baby he knew nothing about. No one had stepped forward to take her off his hands, and there was nowhere he could leave her. Everyone in the district was working hard, searching for bodies and lost objects from the ship, or hoping, by some miracle, to find a survivor clinging to a piece of wreckage.

The women at Otara Station were sympathetic and helpful. They'd put together a bag of food for him, one that was more appetizing than his usual fare, and added tins of condensed milk for the baby and some Dutch rusks he could use for pap by soaking them in a little of the condensed milk, or dry if the baby seemed to be getting new teeth and wanted to chew on something. They'd loaded an old haversack with hard cheese, bread and newly harvested apples and pears and he thought he could manage a few days on that, bolstered with some replacement tins of sardines and hard tack.

Charles Brunton, Mrs. Brunton's son, a large, jovial man with larger feet had given him an old pair of boots, comfortably stretched Bluchers, the nails in the soles almost worn away. He told Frank he purchased himself a new pair of boots for the farm every year, and saved the old ones for any of his workers who might need them, and whose feet were the right size. Sometimes a farm hand who didn't fit a pair would stuff them with newspaper, knowing that he was getting a better pair of shoes than he could afford himself.

Mrs. Brunton had found a dress and a soft blanket for the baby, and slipped Frank a flask of brandy for emergency use; if he couldn't get her to sleep, he was instructed to dip a twisted corner of a handkerchief into the brandy and let her suck on it.

"Always worked for my little ones," said Mrs. Brunton. "Never had a bad night's sleep from any of them, and the boys all grew up to be hard working, honest young men. Look at Charles! He's a Justice of the Peace and a farmer, and he works very hard."

Frank thought about Grace Burns, who had rubbed laudanum on her baby's gums to terrible effect, and decided he would not give the brandy to the baby. He might have a nip or two himself, however.

He shared an evening meal with the family and farm hands, and was sent to the shearing shed to find a place to sleep. Mrs. Brunton recommended that he climb up to the loft and find a spot between the few bales of wool that remained there, shearing season being over for the year.

By then he was exhausted. The shed was full of shearing equipment with few spots to sleep, so after a quick look around he took her advice and climbed the ladder to the loft above the back of the shed; gaps at either end let in a cool breeze and dispersed the lingering scent of lanolin and the faint stench from the boiling down shed nearby. He found a space between two bales of wool, sat down and laid the child beside him. Her eyes opened immediately and she watched him, seeming to wonder why they were there. After two minutes, she made a complicated move, rolling onto her front and raising herself up on her knees. Then she moved one leg and flipped around on her bottom, and said softly, "Mama?"

"Mama's not here, but we'll find her soon, don't worry," he said, remembering the frozen woman on the gate, floating in on the waves with the child held tightly in her arms.

She looked at him trustingly, and raised her arms towards him. He picked her up and circled the limited space, talking nonsense, telling her about Sarah Jane, and how one day they might be friends. She listened with her thumb stuck in her mouth, saying mama every now and then; eventually her eyes closed and her head flopped forward onto his shoulder.

"I've always been good at boring women to sleep." Frank

patted her on the back. "Now, let's get you down. Stay asleep all night, if you don't mind. I'm as tired as hell."

He made a nest for her with some straw and flopped down beside her. It occurred to him that she must have a name, and that he should try to find out what it was. Or give her one for now. How old was she? Older than Sarah Jane, who could not say mama, although she had mastered an m sound with her lips closed and much concentration. Sarah Jane could not do what this child had just done, either: move from her back to a seated position in three awkward moves. She must be older than six months, although she was the same size as Sarah Jane. Nine months, perhaps. His knowledge of what babies could do began and ended with Sarah Jane. Mette's sister, Maren, had several children, and all he knew about their development was that one minute they were babes in arms, the next minute they were running around the yard playing British Bulldog or leap frog.

The child — whatever her name was — was lying on her back with her arms above her head, like someone who'd been told to bail up by a robber, her head turned to one side, her lips slack. He watched her, trying to think of a name for her, and remembered the book he'd seen Mette pull out on the ship, one she'd read before. Was it *The Old Curiosity Shop?* He couldn't remember. But what was the name of the heroine in that book? Mette had told him about the young girl, sniffling and brushing away tears when she died. Little Nell. That was it. He didn't like the sound of that one. How about something similar but stronger? Helen, for Helen of Troy? The face that launched a thousand ships — appropriate. Or Eleanor? That was more like it. Eleanor, after Eleanor of Aquitaine, the crusading queen of England and France. He took a swig of brandy and lay back and thought about what he was going to do to get this child to safety, and to get rid of the burden of carrying her around.

He was awoken in the night by a sharp, pointed pressure on his chest like someone had stabbed him with a blunt knife. He rolled away and sat up, ready for a fight. The baby was next to him, standing, cooing at her accomplishment. She'd used his chest to push herself to her feet.

He rubbed his eyes and yawned. What time was it, for god sakes? "You thinking of going somewhere?"

She took a tottering step forward and then stopped, her arms windmilling, her face a picture of concentration. He watched, grinning. "Persistent little thing, aren't you?"

She took another jerky step forward, and then another; he realized with horror that she was heading for the drop at the edge of the loft, about to step into space.

He edged towards her, trying not to frighten her. She looked at him proudly, and rocked forward.

"Eleanor. Don't move."

He thought he saw her raising her eyebrows quizzically; Eleanor? Don't be silly. He tried again.

"Nelly. Stay still. Don't move." She turned her head towards the drop in front of her, concentrating on her next move.

"Helen…"

As her knee moved upwards he lunged forward, catching her dress as she was about to disappear, swinging her hard against the ladder. She hung beneath him, her bottom lip quivering, before he managed to drag her back up. The quivering lip turned into sobbing. "Come on, Helen," he said, having decided Helen worked best for him, because of the similarity to hellion. "You'll wake everyone up."

He circled the small space again, holding her against his shoulder and patting her back until she calmed down. She'd fallen back to sleep when he heard a sound from below: the creak of a door opening. Keeping in the shadows, he peered over the edge of the loft. A man had entered and was easing the door closed, crouching and looking around the shed as he did so. Obviously, he wasn't there for honest purposes.

He put Helen back in her nest and squatted beside the top of the ladder. Whoever it was appeared to be searching the shed, peering around the machinery and checking over his shoulder like he didn't want to be seen. A shaft of moonlight lit up the intruder suddenly, and Frank realized he was holding something in his hand — a wrench or an axe, by the look of it. He watched for several minutes, growing more suspicious, and then quietly pulled the ladder up into the loft and onto the floor. As he dragged it away from the edge, it scraped against the boards with a loud screech; the intruder spun around and looked up in his direction. He moved back quickly, but was sure the intruder had seen him. He looked familiar, but Frank was not sure where he had seen him before.

He had not brought his revolver with him on the trip, but the intruder didn't know that.

Sounding as confident as he could, he said, "Don't come any closer or I'll shoot your knee out." He always found it best to be specific when he threatened anyone. For some reason, telling someone you were going to shoot was not as convincing as telling them where you were going to shoot them.

The intruder did not reply, but retreated slowly out of the shed, his eyes fixed on the darkness of the loft. As he backed through the open doorway he was briefly illuminated in the moonlight — a flash of fair hair and the upright stance and squared shoulders of an ex-soldier: the man he'd seen coming up the gangplank of the *Tararua* as he escorted Mette to the train. At the time he'd assumed the man was with the mother and child ahead of him — Helen and her mother, as he now believed. But if that were the case, and if he was looking for the child, why hadn't he said anything? It wasn't as if Frank was reluctant to give her up. Perhaps it was just a coincidence, and he was not aware that the child was here with Frank.

He propped the ladder along the edge of the loft, and fixed it in place with four bales of wool. The ladder would give way if anyone tried to climb over it; the barrier would also prevent Helen from using her newfound walking skills to step into the abyss. He lay back beside her and closed his eyes, not sleeping, worrying about what had just happened. An attempted robbery, or something else? He wasn't worried about himself. He could handle a man like that. But with Helen in the way he'd be more cautious, and therefore more likely to be caught out.

It was barely daybreak when the sheep station came to life the next morning. He lowered the ladder and carried the drowsy Helen down to the farm kitchen, where the women were bustling around, looking like they'd been up for hours. An elderly man sat in one corner supervising them. He had a blanket over his lap, and was obviously in poor health.

Mrs. Brunton poured him a cup of strong tea from a pot that was warming on the hob, and handed him a plate. "Help yourself to breakfast from the sideboard, Sergeant. Be quick, because when the men arrive the food will go in a flash. Give the baby to Mary. She'll feed and change her while you're eating."

He'd forgotten about the changing part. "Do you have a spare napkin I can use for the baby? I think she's done something in the one she's wearing."

"I'll get you a fresh one. I don't think you'd be able to master the tuck we use to keep the towel in place. Just fold it into three, put it between her legs, and pull the pilch over it. That'll keep it in place. I'll give you an extra pilch as well. I have a knitted one that I used for Charles when he was a baby."

"And how often do I need to change her?"

"Whenever she's dirty." Mrs. Brunton smiled. "My goodness, Sergeant Hardy. Don't you pay attention to your wife when she's changing your daughter?"

He had to admit he hadn't paid much attention. Who knew it was such hard work to care for a baby?

"Sit by my husband, if you don't mind." She indicated to the man in the corner. "He needs to speak to another man who doesn't spend his life with sheep. I'm off to the beach in a few minutes and he gets lonely when I'm gone all day."

Frank pulled a chair up beside Mrs. Brunton's husband and introduced himself.

"Your wife and son are doing a wonderful job with the survivors."

He nodded, his face sad. "Yes, I'd like to be out there with them myself, but as you can see my health is not good. I was about to leave for Christchurch to speak with the doctors at the hospital there, but unfortunately I've had to delay the trip."

Charles Brunton arrived while Frank was still eating, stuffing himself with bacon and sausages to prepare his body for a few days of near starvation. Charles Brunton was a young, sturdy farmer, with the ruddy cheeks of a man who spent most of his time outdoors. He helped himself to a plate of sausages, eggs and fried bread, and sat down next to Frank.

"I'm off into Fortrose with my wagon this morning. Would you like to come? You can catch the coach to Bluff later today. You'd be there before midnight and there are hotels at the port. You might even get a berth on a ship going back to Bluff from Fortrose, if you could tolerate that."

"Thank you. I'll ride with you to Fortrose and see what I can find."

"I need to load the wagon first. You can help me with that."

"Are you taking in more food for the searchers and survivors?"

Brunton stopped chewing and took a swig of tea. "Not this time. I'm taking in some coffins. I have a carpenter here, and he spent the day yesterday putting five together. He'll keep making them as long as they're needed. They're burying the survivors out on Slope Point, near where the ship was wrecked. On my father's land, actually. They're calling the spot Tararua Acre."

With the coffins loaded, Frank took freshly fed and changed baby from Mary and joined Brunton on the seat of the wagon. Helen settled on his knee like she belonged there, but Frank pressed a rusk into her hand to keep her occupied. The trip promised to be bumpy and slow along the rutted dirt road to Fortrose he could see stretching before them, especially when he compared it to the speed of the mail coach he'd once driven. Of course, the coach had been pulled by a team of Percherons, and the wagon made do with a pair of bullocks who moved at roughly the same speed as an old man walking at his fastest. His fingers itched to have a whip and two large horses in front of him. Add Mette to the picture and it would all be wonderful. He couldn't wait to see her again, and not just because he wanted to rid himself of the burden of the child.

As they entered Fortrose, Helen threw away the now soggy rusk, sniffing sadly. He turned her towards him and spoke nonsense until she settled down again, letting her tug on his beard, and bite his finger.

"Looks like I'm a bit late," said Brunton. "There goes a load of bodies heading out to the burial site now. I should have gone right there instead of coming to Fortrose."

Frank glanced up, but the wagon with the bodies had disappeared. "Are there more bodies stored somewhere?"

"They're keeping them in the goods shed on the jetty. Are you looking for someone?"

Frank thought of William Sampson, floundering in the water and begging for Frank's help to climb on the gate. Had he survived, or had he drowned? Come to that, what had happened to Hinton, or to McNab, the third man he'd not yet identified. Chances are they were all dead, and had taken the secret of the gold to the bottom of the ocean with them.

"There are three men I'd like to know about. Hinton, Sampson and McNab. I was following them in relation to the gold robbery last year."

Brunton shook his head. "Don't know about Hinton or Sampson. But William McNab was at my place yesterday. He came in after dinner and I sent him out to the small storage shed to sleep. He was gone this morning."

"Someone came into the shearing shed in the middle of the night. But he seemed to be looking for something and he had an axe or a wrench in his hand."

"Hmm. Fair haired fellow? About my age?"

"That was him. Did he ask you anything strange?"

"He asked if anyone else was staying here, and I told him the sergeant who'd rescued the baby was out in the shearing shed, so he should keep away from there as the baby would need her sleep. He was looking for his sister."

So the third man - McNab - was the man who had come into the shearing shed last night. He was probably reacting to "sergeant." If he was the criminal who Frank now thought he was, he'd be wary of anyone with the title of sergeant. But what had he come to do in the shearing shed? And why was he carrying a weapon? Had he talked to Hinton or Sampson, and therefore had heard that Frank was after them? That was the only possible explanation.

At least he now knew what the third man looked like, and that he was alive. The next thing to do was to discover what had happened to the other two suspects.

He said goodbye to Brunton, who was heading for the general store to get himself a drink, and walked around the small town, keeping an eye out for either Hinton or Sampson, but not expecting to find either of them walking around. He was sure they were both dead.

A group of police officers had just arrived from Invercargill on horseback and were eating a quick meal outside the general store. They had several pack horses with them as well as their own mounts; no doubt they would be searching for valuables along the coast before the hoards of scavengers arrived to scoop everything up. There must have been several mail sacks on the ship, and he remembered the captain saying they were carrying silver bullion, although that would have gone to the bottom. He wondered how the captain had fared. Drowned, no doubt. He'd said he intended to stay on the ship until the end, and the end had come so suddenly he could not have survived.

After a lap or two of Main Street, he returned to the jetty and found the temporary mortuary. He went inside cautiously, expecting to be shocked. He had to take Helen with him, but he held her facing away from the bodies — not that she'd understand what she saw anyway.

The shed was filled with bodies wrapped in canvas, laid out in two rows, the canvas folded down on the corner of each to expose the upper bodies for identification. Kerosene lamps had been placed at intervals causing shadows to dance on the walls like evil spirits watching over the dead. He made his way slowly along the rows, looking for anyone he recognized. He found the stewardess, Miss Aitken, lying peacefully, her hands crossed on her chest, her hair still pulled back in a tight bun, looking like she was prepared to start work. He patted her on the shoulder, thinking it would help, then recoiled when one arm, still dressed in the shipping line costume, fell away. It had been torn off at the shoulder. He wondered what horror she had endured to lose an arm in the water and how it came to be reunited with her body.

He took a deep breath and continued on. The next person he recognized was one of the clergymen he'd seen on the wharf in Wellington. Someone had placed a bible on his chest, and he, too, looked like someone who was about to start work. In fact, he looked like he would begin a lecture if anyone awoke him.

Right next to the clergyman he found Helen's mother. He held Helen against his chest so she couldn't see, but she was preoccupied with one of his shirt buttons and didn't notice. The mother was still wearing her silver bracelet and he slipped it off. He may need it to provide identification at some point.

He was the only person who could connect Helen and her mother.

At the end of the first row of bodies, he found William Sampson. His clothing was damp, indicating that he'd been placed there recently. Frank squatted beside him, made sure no one was looking, and checked his pockets. In one, he found a small key — not the key to the bullion room, which had been much larger. The other pockets were empty. He took the key and slipped it in his trouser pocket, jiggling Helen awkwardly as he did so. She had managed to get her face against his shirt, and transfer a blob of dirt to her nose. He wiped it off with his sleeve, which was somewhat clean.

Well, that was it then. One gold robbery suspect dead, the other somewhere in the district, and the third, Hinton, who knew where, although probably dead. But until he saw the body Frank wasn't counting on it.

He came out of the gloomy shed and into bright sunlight, wondering what he should do next. A horse ridden at full gallop came from the direction of Waipapa, a woman in the saddle whipping it on. She slowed as she approached, pulling back on the reins, and he realized it was Mrs. Brunton. She kept astride the horse, the reins pulled tight to keep the horse in place. It was a lively one, he could see.

"Thank the Lord I found you, Sergeant Hardy."

He gestured in the direction her son had gone. "Your son just left. He went to the general store."

"I was at the beach near the wreck and I met your wife and daughter."

"Mette?" His heart leapt. She was close? Thank god.

"It's not good news, I'm afraid. She was just arrested by two policemen from Dunedin."

95

"Arrested? For what?"

Mrs. Brunton looked grim. "Kidnapping."

"Kidnapping who? Sarah Jane? Surely not."

"A baby was kidnapped in Dunedin, and one of the police-men, who claims to be an Assistant Commissioner of Police, although I have my suspicions about that, had been following your wife on the train from Dunedin. It's all nonsense, of course. Look, Sergeant, you don't have much time. They've sent her off to the lockup in Invercargill with a couple of oafs who were the only men available. Give me the baby and go after them. Rescue your wife and daughter and bring them back to Otara. We'll hide you until we can work out what to do."

"You think I should follow them on foot?"

She jumped down from the horse and thrust the reins at him. "Take Nightingale. She's made for you. She's a man's horse. I have trouble reining her in." She took Helen from Frank. "I'll take the baby and we'll find Charles at the store. He'll take us home."

"Are you sure? I can't take…she's a Hanoverian, isn't she?"

She glared at him. "Take the bloody horse. She belongs to my husband and he doesn't need her. I'll see you at the house later today. Go!"

He leapt on the horse and spurred it towards the Bluff road. Mette had been arrested and he had to get her back. Too bad he hadn't brought a gun with him. Without it he'd have to rely on his hands and his strength. And his rage.

10

The Rescue

Mette felt like she was in a tumbrel on the way to the guillotine. She sat in the wagon bed, her back pressed against a sharp board on the side, her hands shackled in front of her with a pair of stiff metal handcuffs that cut into her wrists. Sarah Jane lay against her leg, propped up with a sack, drooling as she slept, and twitching when she dreamed about something exciting. Mette was desperate to hold her, but if she made a move, one of the two men escorting her to Bluff would spin around and snarl at her. She'd tried that already. The younger man had threatened to make her walk behind the cart on a rope, like a prisoner on a road crew.

When they had pushed her on board the wagon, she had been terrified they would separate her from her baby. But they'd loaded Sarah Jane beside her like a sack of potatoes, saying they knew the baby wasn't hers, but they needed to get her back to her parents who were on their way from Dunedin to Invercargill by the Mail Coach.

"But she is mine." She hoped the parents of the other baby would realize that Sarah Jane was not the baby that had been stolen from them. But what if they didn't care? What if they were happy to take her lovely daughter away to replace theirs? How would she ever prove she was her mother? Sarah Jane had been born in a hideaway on their farm up near Feilding, and only Frank and three boys had watched the birth. And since then she had moved to Wellington where no one knew her. She didn't know if Frank had even registered the birth, so much else had been going on.

The two men escorting her to Invercargill, a constable and a sergeant from the Otago Police Force, were the only people available to take her there, and the detective who had arrested her had allowed them to do the job with reluctance. Mr. Smith wasn't with them because he had something important to do, he said. He'd told the men to be extra careful with the baby, as it was important she arrived in Invercargill unscathed.

"I know you have some fondness for the child," he said to Mette. "So please take care of her. The men will let you feed her if she cries."

"Of course I'll take care of my own bloody daughter."

He shook his head and sighed, and she knew she should not have sworn at him. All she had achieved was to prove to him she was a criminal. Decent women did not swear.

What had upset her more than anything was realizing that she'd passed Frank as she left Fortrose with Mr. Smith on the wagon loaded with corpses. She'd seen him, but had decided that it wasn't him because he was holding a baby. And now Mrs. Brunton had told her he'd rescued a baby from the wreck and was carrying her around until he found some relatives to take her off his hands. If she had not been under arrest she would have laughed about the misunderstanding.

Sarah Jane awoke, whimpering and scratching her fingernails against Mette's skirt.

"I have to feed my baby," she said.

The younger of the two men, the constable, turned and eyed Sarah Jane. He was almost bald, in spite of his youth, and had a scraggly beard that didn't help his appearance. He was thin and stooped, and a bigger contrast to Frank than you would ever find. Everyone made her think of Frank at the moment, even an ugly man like him, or the other man, the sergeant, who was large and pompous with a big grey beard and stains on his clothing. Mr. Smith must have been short of men to send these two with her.

The constable turned away and spoke over his shoulder, "She can wait. We'll be at the river soon. You can feed her while we're getting on the ferry."

"Can I hold her until then?"

He shook his head dismissively. "Nope. She doesn't need you. She'll survive."

Sarah Jane reached for Mette, her lips mouthing her usual ma ma. Mette's heart was breaking. "Please," she begged the constable. "Mr. Smith said…"

The constable ignored her.

A tear rolled down her cheek. She sniffed and raised her shackled hands together to wipe it away. As she did, she noticed that the lock on the handcuff had not engaged properly. It was an Adams single lock, the kind Frank used to carry when he was an investigator. If she could flip the lock open all the way without disturbing the two men she could remove the handcuffs and hold Sara Jane for a few minutes. If nothing else, she would feel more comfortable, and maybe she could think of a way to escape. She imagined running back down the road holding Sarah Jane, and meeting Frank coming in the other direction. It was a comforting fantasy.

She worked away at the lock, pushing at it with her thumb nail. After several minutes, it snapped open and the two sides of the cuff separated. She waited until the wagon was passing over a bridge, where any noise would be drowned out by the rush of the water, and threw the cuffs into the river. The sergeant had another pair on his belt. She'd seen them. But she would worry about that later. For now, she had her Sarah Jane. She picked her up and hugged her, crying again.

Through her tears, she saw a shape approaching fast. She could not believe what she was seeing. Wasn't that Frank on a huge, pale-grey horse, looking like the Young Lochinvar in Sir Walter Scott's wonderful poem? Was she dreaming? No, it was really him.

Afraid to alert the two men, she whispered into Sarah Jane's ear softly. "Daddy's coming."

He caught up to the wagon and passed by, one finger to his lips. He was not carrying the baby she had heard about, which was just as well. A baby would be terrified to be taken on such a horse. She hoped he hadn't left her somewhere by herself, even temporarily, while he came to save them.

She was filled with joy. He was not only alive, which she knew already, but right here about to rescue her from these horrible men.

She considered what he might do, and decided he'd probably find a better place up ahead and stop them somehow. Maybe at the river, although there'd be other people there. She peered round between the men. They were on a flat, grassy plain, with no place for him to hide, but in the distance she could see that the land dropped away. Perhaps that was where the river was. He'd be down there, somewhere, waiting between the trees.

The horses slowed, and she could feel the road going downhill. Stumpy, windblown trees began to appear on either side of the road. As the trees became larger she waited for something to happen. Surely he would jump out from behind a tree soon, likc a highwayman. He would ask them to stand and deliver.

She had almost given up hope, when he landed beside her in the back of the wagon. He'd dropped down from an overhanging tree branch. Without stopping to say anything, he grabbed the young constable under the armpits, lifted him from his seat, and threw him off the wagon. The constable screamed in a decidedly feminine way, and Mette watched as he landed on his feet beside the wagon, ran a few ungainly steps, and then fell face down on the metalled road. The sergeant was another matter, and resisted as Frank tried to push him from his seat. The pair of them locked together in a bear hug, each trying to throw the other off the wagon.

Mette heard a sudden noise, and turned from watching Frank and the police sergeant wrestling on the seat. The constable had managed to regain his feet and his composure and was running after the slowing cart, his arms flailing around like a windmill. As they were no longer moving very quickly, he soon reached the wagon and grabbed the tailboard. He ran a few steps in that way, then began to pull himself up, his face bright red with exertion. Mette put Sarah Jane at a safe distance from her father, and edged towards the constable. This was something she'd done before and she knew she needed to wait for the perfect moment. When he was half way up on the wagon, with one hand flat on the floorboard and the other holding something below, balancing as if he were on a seesaw, she grabbed his wrist and pulled up as hard as she could and watched as he flew backwards, looking at her in a surprised way until he hit the road behind them again.

This time he did not get up, but stayed seated, receding in the distance.

She could see they were nearly at the river. The ferry was coming across from the far side and would arrive before they did.

She picked up Sarah Jane and held her close, watching in case the two men tumbled on top of them. "Better hurry, Frank. There are people waiting for the ferry."

The sergeant bared his teeth and managed to push Frank back towards the wagon bed. "Better give up, you bastard. And you're under arrest. Anything you say…"

"Has he got any cuffs, Mette?" Frank said, his teeth clenched.

She knelt behind them and reached for the cuffs, holding on to Frank's knee for balance. "Here they are. They're Adams Single Lock. I've got the key from his pocket."

He grunted his thanks. "See if you can slap one on his wrist." He bent the sergeant in Mette's direction, both of them red with exertion, and she hooked one of the circles around his wrist. The sergeant was distracted for minute, shaking his hand to rid himself of the cuff. In one move, Frank threw him backwards and hooked the second circle of the handcuffs around the strut of the seat so that he was stretched across the seat on his back like a cast sheep.

Frank fell back into the bed of the wagon beside Mette and grinned at her. "Well done."

The whip was just a few inches from the sergeant's hand and they could see him straining to reach it with his free hand. Frank picked it up and tossed it on the back of the wagon, then lay across the sergeant's body, his own body pushing the policeman down, and unleashed the horses, watching as they trotted away, freed from their restraints, the reins dragging behind them. "That'll keep you for a bit."

"You're not going to get away with this. Assistant Commissioner Smith will track you down and have your guts for gaiters."

"Commissioner?" asked Mette. "I thought he was a private investigator."

"Not him." The sergeant was twisting his hand, trying to free himself from the cuff on his wrist. "Assistant Commissioner Smith is the nephew of one of the most important men in Dunedin. He won't want this escape to ruin his reputation. He'll track you until he finds you, just see if he doesn't."

Frank picked up Sarah Jane. "Let's go, Mette. Pay no attention to this cretin."

The wagon had come to a stop, and they jumped easily to the ground. Mette had been dying to hug Frank, and she did now, throwing her arms around him and Sarah Jane. "I thought you were dead. *Min gut*, Frank, I didn't know what I was going to do without you."

The constable had appeared in the distance, limping towards them.

"We'd better get out of here." Frank whistled and a huge, pale grey horse appeared from the trees and trotted towards them. "This is Nightingale. Mrs. Brunton lent her to me." He jumped on the horse and helped Mette and Sarah Jane up in front of him. It felt so right to Mette. It was the first time the three of them had been on a horse together, but it was a very big horse and she was sure it could manage their combined weight.

"Where will we go? You heard what that man said about Mr. Smith. He'll be looking for us."

"Let him. We're going to cut across overland west of Fortrose to the Otara Road, and then take that road to Otara Station. Mrs. Brunton has promised to hide us until we can work out what's going on."

"She's such a nice person," said Mette. "But why would she hide us from the police? Are you sure she's not going to turn us in?"

"She's a decent Yorkshire lass who doesn't want some whippersnapper pushing her around," said Frank. "At least, I think so. I'll trust anyone who lets me use a horse like this with no conditions. And she told me her father-in-law was a coachman. He probably knew my father."

Mette leaned back on Frank and closed her eyes, feeling his warmth through his shirt. He never felt the cold. "What's a whippersnapper?"

He shrugged. "I don't know. It's something my father used to say."

He spurred the horse into a fast trot.

By the time they reached the Otara Road she was feeling safe again. The road was heavily treed at the junction, and as they turned into it, they met a young man on horseback trotting towards them.

"Be careful what you say," Frank murmured. "Let's pretend we're on our way to visit your relations in Tokanui. If he asks the name, say Jensen. Let's keep it simple."

"And if it gets awkward, I'll act like I'm stupid," said Mette. Most English men were quite willing to consider a young Scandinavian woman stupid; it played into their preconceptions.

The young man nodded to them. "Are you on your way to the

wreck?"

Frank squeezed Mette's waist, warning her not to say anything. "We heard there'd been a wreck, but we're on our way to Tokanui to stay with relatives."

"In that case, you missed the turn," said the man. "You can turn left off the next track you come to and that will get you there."

"Ah. We'll take that then. Thank you."

The young man had reined in his horse, eager to talk. "I've come from Waikawa. We need help there. So much wreckage is coming ashore from the *Tararua* we can't keep up with it. And bodies as well. Two so far, but there'll be more in the next week."

"Waikawa?"

"It's about twenty miles from the point, further north. Porpoise Bay, if you know the area."

Frank shook his head. "I don't know the area at all. We're from...from Greymouth on the West Coast. We took a ship from Hokitika to Bluff and we're riding up to Tokanui, or we thought we were."

So much for keeping it simple, Mette thought. "You found bodies? How awful. How did they get that far?"

"The tide took them," he said. "One was a young boy of about twelve with gashes on his leg. Looked like a shark got to him."

Mette heard Frank make a sound she'd never heard from him before.

"And a powerful-looking man with red hair and red whiskers who was naked except for his drawers hanging around his ankles. The sea pulls off the clothing, you know, especially trousers."

She heard Frank sigh. "I suppose someone will identify them

eventually. There must be bodies all up and down the coast. Dreadful."

He nodded, and rode away, apparently not suspecting anything. By now, Sarah Jane was letting Mette know she wanted to be fed. They stopped, and she sat on a fallen log and unbuttoned her dress as Frank paced up and down, thinking.

"That's two of them then," he said eventually.

"Two of whom?"

"Of the three men I was following, two are most likely dead, and one is alive. I spoke to William Sampson on the ship after you left. And this morning I found his body in the goods shed in Fortrose. Last night at Otara Station, a man came into the shearing shed where I was sleeping, holding a hammer; he looked as if he wanted to harm somebody. Me, I'm guessing. Charles Brunton told me his name was William McNab, another one of the suspects on the list I was given in Wellington. So he's still alive. That just leaves one more suspect; Robert Hinton, the American. I think he's the man they found on the beach up in Porpoise Bay — the man with red whiskers. Red hair isn't very common. I saw Hinton on the ship. He had very red hair."

Mette was puzzled. "One of your suspects is an American with red hair and whiskers. In that case, it can't be his body at Porpoise Bay. He was on the train from Port Chalmers to Dunedin with me yesterday. And today he was on the train again, on his way to Bluff. I'm sure it's the same person. Not many people have red hair, and I doubt there are two Americans with red hair in the entire South Island."

11

The Shepherd's Hut

Sarah Jane was asleep when they rode up to the Brunton homestead; Mette leaned back against Frank with her eyes closed, but with a tight hold on the baby. He held them both close to his chest, breathing in their scent, relieved and happy to have his family with him again. Mette's arrest meant nothing, really. They'd sort everything out and head to the Bluff, turn Hinton in to the police, and get the reward. Mette would send for Professor Mann's manuscript from the post office in Fortrose and translate it, and they'd be flush with cash for the rest of the year.

He hated being broke. When Colonel Roberts had asked him if he was interested in following the suspected gold robbers, he'd been at the point of returning to the card tables to improve their circumstances. Honest labour hadn't been working, and his horse farm up near Feilding had become a financial bog. The manager he'd hired was doing his best, but he was a new chum from England, not yet used to the ways of New Zealand. Two horses had died of the strangles, and Dead Shot's offspring hadn't been as successful as he'd expected. The filly looked good, but she had the wrong personality for a race horse. Too timid. He'd seen it before — offspring that didn't take after their parents.

They rode up the dusty, poplar-lined driveway to the Brunton homestead, through a display of leaves that had turned yellow as autumn closed in.

The sound of hammers echoed down from the house, and a man in a carpenter's leather apron could be seen in the yard, a pile of coffins beside him. Mr. Brunton sat nearby in a bath chair offering suggestions. Charles Brunton passed them in his wagon, heading towards the site of the wreck with a load of coffins. He nodded at them and continued on without speaking.

Mrs. Brunton came from the house to greet them, holding Helen, who looked much cleaner than she had when Frank had passed her to Mrs. Brunton in Fortrose. Mrs. Brunton's face showed the stress of the past few days. She probably hadn't slept much, and had heard too many heart-breaking stories; the strain of it all was written on her face.

"He's been here. And he says he's coming back. My husband spoke with him, and told him we'd not seen either of you. Lied with a straight face, my husband did, and he's a Justice of the Peace. Mind you, I told him if he spoke a word about you being here, Sergeant, he could expect to sleep on the kitchen floor tonight."

Frank slid off the horse and helped Mette and Sarah Jane down.

"Who's been here?" Mette asked. "Who are you talking about?"

"Smith. The man who arrested you," said Mrs. Brunton. "I

don't know where he's from or who he works for, but I really doubt he's with the police. I asked to see his warrant card and he refused to show it to me. He claimed he'd left it in his room."

"The sergeant taking me to Invercargill told me Mr. Smith is an assistant commissioner," said Mette. "And works for someone very important."

"He's not the assistant commissioner of anything connected to the police," said Mrs. Brunton. "There's a commissioner of police for the whole country, and if he was second-in-command I'd know about it. For some reason this whole kidnapping is important to him. I have the feeling he isn't going to give up. With everything that's going on, you'd think he would join with all the other police arriving in the area. There's so much to be done."

"General Gordon was Assistant Boundary Commissioner to the Border in Crimea when I was there," said Frank. "Smith could be assistant commissioner of something other than the police. What about the policeman he had with him? The one who arrested Mette. How does he fit in?"

"I saw him down at the burial site earlier today. I don't think he knew what was going on. He just believed that Mr. Smith was in a position to tell him what to do."

Mr. Brunton had been listening from his perch near the carpenter, and leaned forward. "I suspect Smith works for the government in some capacity — assistant commissioner of the waterworks or something similar. I doubt he's lying deliberately, he's just implying something he isn't. My wife and I think you should go into hiding until things calm down. He's obviously got some pull."

"What about the real kidnappers. Whose baby did they kidnap, and where are they now?"

"Did you think it might be this baby?" asked Mrs Brunton, jiggling Helen. "She was on the ship from Dunedin, and you told me you saw the mother coming on board. Was it really her mother, do you think?"

Frank considered that possibility. "It'd be too much of a coincidence, I would say. The woman drowned saving this baby. If she wasn't the mother, don't you think she would have tossed Helen away and saved herself? And the man I thought was with her turns out to have been one of my gold robbery suspects. More likely they were on the way to Melbourne with some of the gold, and brought the baby along as cover. Who would suspect a mother and child of being involved in something like that?"

Helen started wriggling in Mrs. Brunton's arms, and reaching out for Frank.

"Did you know she's learned how to walk?" said Mrs. Brunton. "Look at this, Sergeant Hardy."

She set the baby on her feet, held her by her hands until she was steady, and then let her go. Helen wasted no time. She lunged towards Frank and threw her arms around his legs. "Dada."

He picked her up and smiled down at her. "I'm not your father, Helen. I'm Frank. You can call me Frank."

Helen smiled back, seeming to understand. "Fah?"

"Frank," he said. "Frank."

She nodded and grabbed his beard. "Fah."

Frank pulled her hand away. "Good enough. We don't know where your father is, Helen, but Fah will find him. "

Mette gave him an odd look, and he felt a twinge of guilt. He'd spent more time with Helen than he ever spent with Sarah Jane. He'd had no choice with Helen, but even so he should pay more attention to Sarah Jane and not just play with her for a few minutes and hand her back to Mette. He adored his daughter, of course, when she was behaving. As soon as she cried or soiled herself, back she went to her mother. He'd become all too aware of his lack of responsibility, now he'd spent a couple of days taking care of Helen.

"Well, we'll sort Helen's parentage out eventually," said Mrs. Brunton. "For now, you'd better head up to the hiding place we've arranged for you. Give it a day and come back down tomorrow to see if there's any more news."

"Up? Where are we going to hide? In the shearing shed again?"

"Better than that." She pointed towards the hills. "There's a shepherd's hut up there about a quarter of a mile away. You can see the roof from here, poking above the trees at the top of the hill. Follow the track up through the paddock. I've left you enough food for a couple of days, and some blankets. The shepherd is with the flock in the far paddock on the other side of the lake, so he's sleeping rough."

"This reminds me of the soddy," said Frank, when they were settled into the shepherd's hut and tucking in to Mrs. Brunton's supplies. "Bloody uncomfortable, but at least we were together and alone." He grinned at her over a mutton and pickle sandwich. "Not that we're alone now. A bit awkward, isn't it?"

Mette blushed. "I grew up in a house with everyone sleeping in the same room. It wasn't so bad."

Frank took her hand, entwining her fingers with his. "What did you do when your parents...?"

"I put my head under the pillow and blocked my ears."

"No pillows here. Maybe we can throw a blanket over Sarah

111

Jane and Helen."

"We could wait until they go to sleep."

He leaned forward and kissed her. "I have some brandy Mrs. Brunton gave me. We could slip some into their food. Helen anyway. What do you think?"

Mette frowned. "I would never do that. Not after what happened to Grace Burns."

Frank spooned some pap into Helen's eager mouth, while Mette fed Sarah Jane.

"All babies aren't alike, are they?" she said. "Didn't Mr. Smith have a description of the baby? Helen has bright blue eyes, navy blue almost, and Sarah Jane's are dark brown. Their hair is a different colour, and Sarah Jane has an olive complexion, like you. I think Helen is older than Sarah Jane, even though they're about the same size. Actually, when I fed Sarah Jane, Mr.Smith asked what it was like to feed someone else's baby, because she didn't look like me."

"Did you slap him?" asked Frank.

"No, but I swore at him, and that just made him think I was a criminal." She switched Sarah Jane to the other side. "You'd be able to describe Sarah Jane to someone, wouldn't you?"

"I'd say she was beautiful like her mother."

Mette shook her head and looked away from him. He could see she had some doubts about how well he knew his own daughter, so he improvised. "I'd say she has big brown eyes and a mop of auburn hair, and takes after me, except that she's more intelligent than I am, like her mother."

That seemed to do the trick, and they finished with the girls and made a bed for them with blankets and a pile of straw. Within minutes, the two girls were breathing quietly, fast asleep in each other's arms.

Frank pulled Mette to him and leaned over her. "We're alone. Finally."

She stroked his cheek and smiled up at him. "I'm so glad you're alive. When I heard the ship had gone down with a massive loss of life I was ready to die myself."

He said something that had been on his mind since the wreck. "You know, I'm eighteen years older than you, and will probably die first."

"But not yet. Not for another twenty years at least."

"Longer than that, I hope. My father's still alive and he's seventy-seven."

"Thirty-five years. Let's make the most of it then."

He fell asleep draped across Mette's body, her hands on his back, feeling a comfort he hadn't felt for weeks. He was in the middle of a pleasant dream, riding Copenhagen along the ridge of his horse farm with Mette seated in front of him, when he was awoken by an animal of some kind landing on his back. He rolled off Mette and sat up abruptly.

"What was that?"

Mette turned on her side and said sleepily, "What was what?"

"Something fell on me."

Something scratched his back. He rolled away from it. Was an animal in the hut with them? A possum? A rat? A feral dog?

In the dark, he saw a small, dark shape crouched on the dirt floor. The hut had one tiny window and the light that came through was blocked by trees. He moved between the shape and Mette, wondering if he could get to Sarah Jane and Helen without it attacking. If it was a possum, as he suspected, it would be dangerous if it felt threatened. But as his eyes got

113

used to the dark, he realized that the shape was human. Helen.

"For god's sake, Helen. You scared me."

"Fah?" her voice quivered as he picked her up. She put her head on his shoulder and sniffed. "Fah."

"Is something the matter, Helen?"

Mette shuffled around them and gathered Sarah Jane in her arms, and rocked her from side to side to keep her calm.

Frank joined her and copied Mette's motions. Both the girls looked happier, but now he could see down the hill to the yard in front of the Brunton's homestead. A shape crossed from behind the trees and moved towards the shearing shed, followed by two more shapes. One of them, the larger of the two, was holding a lantern, which swung back and forth creating shadows on the out buildings.

He moved back. "Get away from the window, Mette. Someone's in the yard. I think it's your friend Smith and his two thugs."

"What's a thug?"

"It's a word I heard in India. It means…never mind. They're down there and looking for us."

"Will they come up here, do you think? Should we leave."

He took another quick look through the window, and saw the three men staring up towards the shepherd's hut, one with a hand above his eyes. They must be able to see the roof of the hut. "Looks like they're thinking about it. Let's get out of here; we'll take the blankets and food with us so the hut looks uninhabited."

Mette moved Sarah Jane to her hip. "Give Helen to me and you carry everything else."

Helen did not want to go to Mette. She pushed away from

her and said, "Fah. Fah." several times, her voice rising to a crescendo.

Frank took both the girls from Mette. "Hand me the food bag. You take the blankets and your bag."

They eased open the door of the hut, not much more than a gate, really, and edged outside.

The girls leaned away from each other, making them difficult to carry. It wasn't the weight that bothered him, but the slipperiness. It was like trying to carry a couple of eels. "Round the back of the hut and uphill," he said. "We'll get as far away as we can. Once we're on the other side of the hill we'll head down to the road." He looked back towards the yard. In the light from the lantern he saw one of shadows moving in their direction. "Let's go. They're coming."

Behind the hut, a path ran up to the top of the hill through the stunted bush, which disappeared as they reached the crest. On the other side, there were few trees, but generations of sheep had trodden pathways along the hill and down towards the road. Occasionally a cluster of bushes sprang up between the tracks.

They stopped to catch their breath, and both the babies began to cry at the same time. Mette dropped her bundle of blankets and took Sarah Jane from Frank. "Shh, shh. They'll hear you crying."

Sarah Jane put her head on Mette's chest, rooting for her breast. "Can we stop somewhere? If I feed her she'll settle down."

"Let's get down to that patch of bushes down there, and get behind it. You can feed her there. Run."

He grabbed the roll of blankets, juggling them with the bag

of food and Helen, and followed Mette down the hill towards the cluster of bushes. As he flung himself to the other side, dropping Helen and the blankets, he couldn't help noticing Mette was not winded; he was momentarily envious of her youth.

They huddled behind the bush as Mette fed Sarah Jane. He kept an eye on the top of the hill, expecting the three men to appear. Helen started to whimper, and reached for Mette.

"Now you want her." He jiggled Helen, grinning at her foolishly. If she started to cry as Smith and his henchmen came over the hill, they'd hear her.

On cue, Helen began to cry, a loud scream that echoed down the valley from where they were hidden.

"Can you feed her as well?"

Mette bit her lip. "I really don't want to. It would be strange."

"Better than getting caught by Smith."

She stared down at Sarah Jane, and he could see she was upset at the idea. Helen stopped to take a breath, gasping. He could see she was about to start again.

"Sorry Mette, but I have to do this." He took his handkerchief and the brandy from his pocket, opened the bottle, and dipped the folded corner of the handkerchief inside.

Helen opened her mouth for the brandy-soaked handkerchief and sucked it eagerly, her tantrum forgotten.

"You should have let her suck your finger. That works better than brandy," said Mette.

It was a bit late for that information. He leaned forward to see if anyone had come over the crest of the hill, and pulled back hurriedly. One man was standing there, looking around, the moon outlining his body.

"Have a look at the top of the hill," he whispered. "Do you

think that's Smith up there?"

She edged over, trying not to disturb Sarah Jane, and peered around the bush.

"I think so, but it's hard to tell in the dark."

He took another look. The shape had disappeared.

"We should get moving." Sarah Jane had fallen asleep at Mette's breast, and Helen had succumbed to the brandy. "We can leave the blankets and the food under the bush and carry one baby each."

Mette buttoned up her dress, balancing the sleeping Sarah Jane on her knee. "Where should we go? Should we go back to the hut?"

"They must suspect we're there. I think we should head to the burial site and find a real police inspector. Any intelligent policeman will understand. Several people knew that I pulled Helen from the water."

Mette sighed. "I hope so. I'm getting tired of this. I should never have insisted on bringing Sarah Jane."

"This will soon be over, and we can claim the reward," Frank said. "Some of it, anyway. Sampson told me he knew about the gold, and he was travelling with Hinton. I reckon Hinton has it on him."

Mette nodded, but he wasn't sure that she was convinced. She was more optimistic about life than he was, but he was more inclined to rely on luck when money was needed.

At Tararua Acre, an early morning mist wove itself between the newly filled-graves with their wooden markers, and shovels that had been left in the ground for work to continue on a new day. Four holes had been dug, and left covered with tarpaulins. Empty coffins sat near the pathway to the beach, beside a dray covered with a tarpaulin which appeared to hold bodies.

The workers would continue their gruesome work, and would transfer these bodies to coffins, and then into graves when they arrived at daybreak.

The water was at a distance, down a long, grassy slope, but they could hear the repetitive sound of the waves as they crashed on the shore.

"We're too early for anyone, but they'll be here soon." Frank dragged a tarpaulin from one of the graves with one hand and threw it against a mound of dirt, then sat with Helen in the centre. His muscles ached from carrying her, and his shoulders felt cramped. "Let's see if we can get some sleep here until someone arrives. Sit close and we'll keep each other warm."

Mette huddled next to him, with Sarah Jane on her lap. He did not feel as contented as he had when they'd arrived at the Brunton's. A dark feeling of impending doom had seeped over his soul. Something about the graves and the coffins was bothering him, and the smell of death hung in the air. The thought that he'd die before Mette and lie in a grave like this nagged at him in a way that nothing else did.

12

Tararua Acre

Inspector Buckley and his men appeared out of the mist on horseback, riding in a cluster that reminded Mette of a drawing she'd seen of Odin on his eight-legged horse, Sleipner. Or maybe the four horsemen from the Illustrated Bible she'd bought for Joey...but she didn't want to think of that, or what it meant to ride a pale horse, like the one Frank had ridden when he rescued her from the police. There had been so much death on this beach, and she could feel in her body the sorrow that came in with every wave.

She had fed both the girls and changed their napkins, and was holding them close, and keeping them as warm as she could in the cold, grey light of the new day. Frank was walking back and forward along the crest of the slope down to the beach, keeping an eye open for the police, and watching for something to wash up with each wave. She could feel his worry.

The police were followed by a motley group of gravediggers, treasure hunters, and the desperate families of the dead, searching with fading hopes for a sign that their loved one had survived, or, at the very least, been washed ashore and identified. A man in his fifties riding alone in a green, two-wheeled spring cart came last. He stopped near Mette and began to unload his cart, humming softly to himself.

He noticed her on the tarpaulin with the girls, and asked, "Do you mind if I set up my camera beside you? The light's good here, and if I put my equipment on the tarpaulin it will stay clean."

"Not at all." She was interested. She'd seen an image of the Rimutaka train disaster in the newspaper a few months ago, but hadn't known how they did it. It looked like a drawing, but she didn't know if the scene had been copied from a photograph, or was actually a photograph which had been traced and transferred to the newspaper in some way. Either way, it had been very clever and had helped her understand the accident.

"Are you taking a photograph for the newspaper?" she asked.

"That'll be the day." He shook his head. "Photographs in the newspaper? Some say it might happen, but it seems a bit fantastical to me. My partner does a nice woodcut of photographs I take, and sometimes the newspaper publishes those. It's a slow process, though, and not much use if you want to get something in the paper quickly. Very expensive as well."

"You're just taking photographs to sell, then? For people to remember, or who can't be here? I imagine anyone who lost someone would want to know where they were lost."

He took a three-legged stand from his cart and stood it on the ground, moving it around until it was properly balanced. "Artists are painting scenes of that in Invercargill and Dunedin, and making themselves a few quid." He took out what looked like two wooden boxes joined together, one smaller than the other, and fixed them to the top of the stand. "I'm here because the police asked me to take photographs of the victims before they're buried. For identification purposes."

"Ah." That was something she preferred not to know about. What a gruesome job, photographing dead people. She'd seen photographs of parents with their dead children propped up beside them, and it had horrified her: *memento mori*, they were called. Of course, in this case it made sense. How would she have felt if Frank had disappeared and she didn't have a body to bury? A photograph would at least be something to hold on to.

The family members and friends of the lost were walking past the coffins and staring into them, their eyes full of mingled hope and despair. She heard one man exclaim, "That's him. Thomas Bailey. My head waiter."

He wiped the corner of one eye with his little finger and walked over to where Mette sat with the girls. "So sad." He obviously wanted to talk to someone. "I didn't know him well, but he was my head waiter at the Criterion Hotel in Dunedin. I gave him a few days off to visit Invercargill, which I thought he would enjoy, and this is what happened to him. He came from Manchester on holiday with his brother, but his brother returned home a few months ago."

"So he has no relatives in New Zealand?"

The man shook his head and wiped his eyes again, this time with the back of his hand.

"We will all say a prayer over him as he's buried," she said.

He nodded slowly. "They're having a ceremony later, for everyone who's identified today. Prayers are being offered in almost every church in the colony. There were several

Wesleyan clergymen on board. They were on their way to a conference in Melbourne. It seems everyone knew someone who was on the ship. It's a national tragedy."

She smiled sympathetically and went back to entertaining Sarah Jane and Helen with stories they didn't understand. Helen was particularly interested in Hans Christian Anderson's story, *The Princess and the Pea*, and laughed happily when Mette announced in her best queen's voice, "Twenty feather beds!" She lingered on the words, wishing she, too, had twenty feather beds. The tarpaulin was cold and uncomfortable with not a feather in sight.

One of the men who had been checking the coffins wandered towards them, not really looking at them and sighed. "Not there," he said. "Not there."

He was clutching a woman's shawl to his chest, his face blank with misery.

"That's his wife's shawl," said the hotel owner as the man moved away towards the ocean. "He was an Able Bodied Seaman on the ship and his wife and child were with him on the voyage. The captain directed him to get in the life boat — the one that put out to sea and met the *Kaikanui* — and he knew he couldn't refuse to go; it was his duty. So he lashed his wife to the mast with her shawl, and gave her his watch and all his money. Now all he has left is the shawl, which he found in the seaweed yesterday. He's searching for his wife and child, but they probably went down with the ship."

Mette stared at him, too overcome with sadness to speak. Thank heavens she still had Frank. How close she had come to losing him.

A dray arrived with more mourners and the hotel owner turned towards it. "I'd best return to Fortrose in the dray and catch the coach to Wyndham," he said. "I'll need to write a letter to Thomas's brother in Manchester and tell him the sad news."

"A pity they don't have the telephone in yet," said the photographer. "I hear they put up a petition in Fortrose to run a line from there to Wyndham." He shook his head. "The modern world. It's very strange, Mrs. Hardy. The next thing you know we'll all be flying by balloon to the moon."

As she watched the hotel owner leave in the dray, she thought of Frank again, imagining herself receiving a letter saying he had gone down with the ship. How horrible that would have been.

She watching him at the top of the slope, and trying to push the negative thoughts from her her mind, when she saw him turn away from the ocean and approach the group of police. The leader dismounted and fell into conversation with him, nodding as Frank gestured towards the beach. At one point, the leader turned and beckoned to a second man, who dismounted and joined them.

When he'd finished talking to the officers, he came over to her. Helen was disgruntled, now that Mette had finished her storytelling, and refused to look at him, burrowing her head into Mette's side, but Sarah Jane reached for him, and he picked her up and hugged her against his shoulder, stroking her hair, until she started to wriggle. He put her back beside Mette. "I think Inspector Buckley's on our side. The detective who arrested you says he's certain that Smith is an official of some kind. But the inspector says he's never heard of anyone named Roderick Smith with any kind of judicial authority."

"He fooled me," said Mette. "Although I thought it more

likely he was a private investigator of some kind. Are the police going to let us go?"

"The inspector wants to talk with the Bruntons first. He says if they're willing to confirm that I pulled Helen from the water after the shipwreck, and if I swear that Sarah Jane is mine, they'll let us go. But he wants us to go to the Bluff and stay there until he's finished here, and keep Helen until he can sort that out. That'll mean a few days in a Bluff hotel for us. I suppose we can manage that. I still have eight quid on me. How much do you have left?"

"Four pounds. Will twelve be enough to get us home?"

He shrugged. "Probably. Depends how long we have to stay in Bluff and wait for Helen's family to claim her." He lay beside her, leaning on one elbow. "The inspector told me someone's coming from Fortrose with food. I hope you can last until they get here. I know you're not used to missing meals like I am."

"I drank some of Helen's condensed milk from your haversack. That will keep me going for now. I used the napkins in your bag for the girls as well. I didn't know you carried napkins around with you."

"Only since I've been stuck with Helen. I didn't know how much work babies were."

She yawned, and Frank squeezed her knee. "Not long now." He looked up at the photographer, who was busy manipulating the two boxes on the stand away from each other, revealing what looked like bellows between them. "Are you here to take photographs of the scene for the hearing?"

"He's going to photograph the bodies for identification." Mette spoke quickly, to forestall another long explanation.

"Here comes the first one now," said the photographer. Two men were carrying an open coffin towards them. "They're

124

going to prop each coffin at an angle in front of the camera and I'll take a photograph of the person inside. The good thing is I won't have to worry about my subjects moving, which is…"

He stopped, realizing Mette wasn't amused, and concentrated on the camera. She could see that the two boxes had rails running between them, along which the bellows were stretched. He pulled a black velvet cloth from his bag as well, and she wondered what he intended to do with it.

Two diggers had stopped in front of them. "Only three unidentified today, Mr. Kebble," one said. "Two men and a boy."

Frank dragged himself to his feet. "Do you need a hand holding them up?"

"This one's light. Just a young lad. Found on the beach at Porpoise Bay. They brought him and the other one down last night with one of the men."

Frank held the side of the coffin and stared in. He was upset, she could tell. "I know this boy," he said. "His name is Tommy. He was the brass polisher. He told me his father works at the wharf in Bluff Harbour and got him the job that way."

The photographer took out a notebook and pencil and jotted something down. "I'll put that information with the photograph. And we'll make sure we let his father know. He shouldn't be hard to find."

Frank helped the men lift the coffin up to a forty-five degree angle. They held it still as the photographer slid the bellows back and forth along the rails.

"I'm changing the focus," he said to Mette. "If the focus is good, the photograph will be clear. I want to make sure his father will recognize him."

125

She felt a sob rise in her throat. Here was a boy who worked at sea in a job that made him feel important, and gave him a chance to help provide for his family. And now his father would be given a photograph of him lying in a coffin. He'd not even see his body. How terrible.

The photographer slid a glass plate into the back of the camera, and ducked under the black velvet cloth he'd thrown over the whole thing. "Hold him still for a count of twenty," he said from beneath the cloth. Everyone froze until the photographer came out from under the cover and smiled. "Done. Next please." He pulled the plate from the camera and placed it carefully in a box at his feet.

Frank touched the boy on the cheek before the two diggers lifted the coffin onto their shoulders, and then followed them to one of the graves. They removed the tarpaulin, put a lid on the coffin, hammered nails into the lid to hold it down, and then passed the coffin to two more men waiting to lower the coffin and cover it with dirt. A minister was standing nearby, ready to say a few kind words to any family members or friends who might be present as the boy was lowered into the grave. But of course there was no one except Frank, who had accompanied the coffin to the grave and bowed his head. She wondered how he knew the boy.

He helped the men load a large body into a second coffin, and joined them in carrying it to the photographer. Mette was not expecting to be upset, knowing this one contained the body of a grown man, which was not as bad as seeing a drowned child. But Frank had looked up at her oddly when he saw the body, as if it might be someone they knew. She waited as they brought it over and tilted it towards the photographer; the man had red hair and whiskers. She put Sarah Jane down on the tarpaulin and went to get a closer look. Then she caught Frank's eye and shook her head. No, it was not Hinton, the red-haired American. Not a bit like him. Frank nodded, understanding, as he always did. They could talk to each other without words, now that they'd been together for more than three years.

By the time the third coffin with its terrible cargo was carried over she was sitting on the tarpaulin playing with the girls. This body would certainly be that of a stranger, and her heart, already broken by seeing the boy, Tommy, would be able to absorb the shock. She was not going to think about all these poor people and the tragedy they and their loved ones had suffered. She would not even look at this one.

But she did. Something made her glance up as the photographer fussed with his camera and the men lifted the coffin into place. She stood slowly and moved closer, wanting to know if her suspicions were correct.

"Frank?"

He was kneeling behind the coffin holding it in place, and didn't hear her.

"Frank?" she said again. "We know this man."

Frank eased the coffin to the ground and looked at the body inside. "Get the inspector," he said to one of the gravediggers. "This man has been murdered." He turned to Mette. "It's McNab."

In the third coffin, his eyes protruding in what looked like terror, was the man she had seen boarding the *Tararua*, following the woman who had drowned holding Helen, both of them with that memorable, straw-coloured hair.

He stared out into the world from which he had recently departed through protruding eyes, his hair standing on end, his head raised from the bottom of the coffin, making it appear as if he were trying to get out. His shirt was open, revealing a mottled purple mark on his neck.

Inspector Buckley hurried up, looking weary. "What have you found, Sergeant? How do you know he's been murdered?"

"This is William McNab, a suspect in the gold robbery from the *Tararua* last year. I saw him at Otara Station the night after the ship went down, so I know he survived the sinking. And he hasn't been dead long. Look at the position of his head."

Inspector Buckley nodded, and leaned into the coffin, his face close to McNab's. He felt around his jaw and neck. "Turn him on his side, Hardy. Be careful. There might be blood."

Frank obeyed. The inspector knelt and inspected McNab's back. "All the way, now. Easy. I can't see a wound, and I can't smell any poison. I would say by the mark on his neck he's been strangled, but I'll have to wait for the autopsy results to be sure." He raised one of the legs and bent and straightened it. "*Rigor mortis* has set in on his jaw and shoulders, but hasn't reached his lower body yet. What time did you say you saw him?"

"The middle of the night," said Frank. "On the night before last. He came into the shearing shed where I was sleeping with the baby; he was carrying a hammer or an axe, and I thought he intended to attack me. He could have been murdered any time between then and now."

"He wasn't here yesterday," said the photographer. "Mr. Brunton brought these coffins down in the late afternoon, and I was here until dusk. He must have been put under the tarpaulin on the dray overnight."

The inspector eyed Frank, pulling at his beard, looking like he was trying to work something out. Mette was worried.

Wouldn't Frank be a suspect if one of the men he'd been following was murdered?

The inspector confirmed her suspicions. "Tell me about what you were doing? Why were you following him? Who hired you for the job?"

"Colonel Roberts of the Armed Constabulary in Wellington asked me to follow three men who were suspects in the gold robbery last year. You can check with him if you like. I saw two of the suspects on the ship after I boarded in Wellington, and this man came aboard in Dunedin. The Constabulary thought the gold might be concealed somewhere in Dunedin, so I suspect he brought it on board with him. It's probably gone to the bottom."

"You saw McNab at Otara Station two nights ago, and he tried to attack you? What would he have to gain from doing that?"

"He didn't try anything, but he was in the shearing shed with a weapon. At the time, I thought one of the other suspects was on to me and had told McNab, but my wife saw that suspect, Robert Hinton, on his way to the Bluff in the train. He hasn't had time to contact McNab and tell him of his suspicions. The third suspect, William Sampson, went down with the ship. I saw his body in Fortrose in the goods shed."

"Can you show me the list Colonel Roberts gave you?"

Frank pulled the list from his pocket and handed it to the inspector. "His name's at the bottom of the page. William McNab. Not that common a name, I don't think."

The inspector spread the crumpled piece of paper on his hand and stared at it intently. He handed it back to Frank. "Take another look at that third name."

Frank looked at it. "What am I supposed to see?"

"William McNay," said the inspector. "Not McNab. That letter is a y not a b."

"William McNay?" said the photographer, who had been following the discussion with interest. "We buried a man with that name yesterday morning. I was going to take a photograph of him, but then we found an old identification card on him. A steward, it said he used to be, on the *Tararua*. He's buried right over there, next to where you put the young lad."

Mette sat up on the tarpaulin, her senses tingling. "If Mr. McNab wasn't the person involved in the gold robbery, doesn't that mean he must have been involved in the kidnapping? And couldn't that mean that Mr. Smith is the person who wants him dead? It must have been McNab they were looking for last night, not us, Frank. Don't you think the Bruntons could be in trouble, inspector?"

13

Frank and the Inspector

Inspector Buckley took the hill to the Brunton's place, gun in hand, moving at military quick time, covering the ground efficiently and fast, like a soldier. Frank followed him up the zigzagging sheep tracks, around the bush where they'd left the food and blankets, and over the hill to the shepherd's hut. His double-time marches up Mount Victoria in Wellington had got him back into fighting condition, but the slope was uneven and difficult to negotiate, and he was breathing hard by the time they arrived at the shepherd's hut. The inspector wasn't winded at all, even though he must be a good fifteen years older than Frank.

Frank was ready for a fight, but Inspector Buckley had turned down his request for a weapon; he felt naked and exposed going in to battle without a gun. Three men with weapons would easily overcome two men with one gun between them. He had grabbed a couple of rocks. Better than nothing, but not much.

From the shepherd's hut they could see the kitchen window of the Brunton homestead. A night lamp was glowing behind the undrawn curtain, although morning had long since arrived. A prudent farm wife like Jane Brunton would not waste kerosene, and she would certainly have pulled the curtains back the minute she entered the kitchen. As they watched, a shadowy figure holding something that looked like a gun moved from one side of the window to the other.

"Someone's there," said the inspector. "Someone who has no business being in that kitchen. Your wife was right."

Frank shaded his eyes and squinted at the house. "That's one of the two men who were taking my wife to the lockup in the Bluff, I think. The larger of the two men."

"I meant to ask you," said the inspector. "How did you get her back?" He pulled back the hammer of his gun. "No. Don't tell me. Best I don't know. Let's go get them."

They crept down the track to the house, staying on the grass to avoid making any unexpected sounds, the inspector with his revolver levelled at the kitchen door.

They stopped in the yard and sheltered behind the shearing shed, watching for a sign they'd been heard.

"The men who took my wife claimed they were police from Invercargill. But they had no proof. They didn't show warrant cards, and they weren't in uniform."

"Oh, they were mine." The inspector grinned apologetically. "A sergeant and a constable. Detective Tuohy chose them because they were useless and he couldn't spare anyone else with more than half a brain. I hope they didn't cause your wife any trouble. Tuohy was convinced she was a kidnapper, you know. It was her blond hair and the baby that made him think so. She matched the description of the female kidnapper."

"My wife was told the police didn't have a good description," said Frank.

132

"There was an off-duty detective playing cricket at the grounds," said Buckley. "And he gave the Dunedin police an excellent description of both of them. They couldn't put that out, of course, but they asked us to be on the lookout for the couple." He raised his gun again and peered over it around the shed. "No movement at all now. At this time of day there should be lots of women bustling around."

"How are we going to do this?" asked Frank. "With only one gun between us."

"We'll check to see if Smith is there, and if he isn't we'll just walk in. I can control my men, misguided as they are."

"How about I go in first by the kitchen door?" said Frank. "I'll distract them, and you can go around through the front door and come up behind them. They might say something to me that they wouldn't say to you."

Inspector Buckley nodded. "That'll work. Give me a chance to get to the other door and go in."

They ran, bent low, to the kitchen window and stopped on either side; the inspector looked inside, then pulled back, shaking his head at Frank. Then he gestured towards the back of the house and left, moving smoothly.

Frank waited five minutes, took a rock from his pocket and held it behind his back as he threw the kitchen door open.

"Sergeant Hardy! Thank the Lord you're here," said Mrs. Brunton. She was wearing her nightdress, her hair in a long braid, sitting bolt upright in a cane kitchen chair, her hands on her knees. She faced her husband who was slumped over, his mouth slack and eyes closed, asleep in his bath chair. The constable and the sergeant Frank had last seen escorting Mette to the gaol in Bluff were standing with guns trained on the pair. Smith was nowhere in sight. "These fools have had us here for hours, and they've locked my women in the larder. They came with Mr. Smith in the middle of the night and woke us up. He left saying…"

He knew she was trying to tell him as much as she could, but she was cut off by the sergeant. "Shut your damn mouth."

Frank experienced a surge of anger. "I wouldn't speak to the lady like that if I were you."

The sergeant sneered at him. "What are you going to do about it? Report me to my superior?"

The constable swung his gun away from Mr. Brunton and waved it at Frank. "I could shoot him, sarge, and say he was trying to break in. We're allowed to do that, aren't we?"

"Seems a bit foolish to me," said Inspector Buckley from behind him. The constable turned his head, leaving his gun dangling in Frank's direction. Frank took the opportunity to knock the gun to the ground with a rock. He picked up the gun from the floor and held it against the constable's head, noticing that it wasn't cocked.

The sergeant moved his gun closer to Mrs. Brunton, eying Frank nervously. "The Assistant Commissioner asked us to keep an eye on these two until he came back," he said to the inspector. "Says they're accessories after the fact in the kidnapping of a baby girl from Dunedin."

"And you believe him?" asked the inspector. "Put down the gun, sergeant. You've been had. Roderick Smith has no authority to hold anyone."

The sergeant lowered his gun, his jaw out. "Detective Tuohy said he was someone important."

"Detective Tuohy has seen the error of his ways. Now, tell me about Smith. Where has he gone? What makes you think he's coming back?"

The sergeant and the constable exchanged glances. "He said he was meeting someone down at the beach," said the constable. "And he told us he'd be back before dawn."

"You do realize it's well past dawn?" The inspector took the sergeant's gun and tossed it to Frank.

Mrs. Brunton was on her feet checking her husband. "He took one of our horses. I heard him go over to the stables, and then I heard him leave."

"He was here earlier looking for us," said Frank. "We saw the three of them in the yard, and we left the shepherd's hut to get away from them."

She frowned. "I don't think he was looking for you, or at least not both of you. When he first got here I heard him say something about finding him." She took a key hanging beside the larder door and unlocked it. "Come on out. It's safe."

Three women trailed out and stood together, arms folded, glaring at the sergeant and the constable.

"That was very unpleasant," one of the women said to the sergeant. "I hope you get locked up in a small space like that yourself and see how you like it."

"Does anyone have any idea who Smith was going to meet?" asked the inspector. "You two, what did he tell you?"

"He found something in one of the sheds," said the sergeant. "He picked it up from the floor. A shipping ticket I think. He spoke to Mr. Brunton about it. I didn't hear what they said, though."

The discussion had awoken Mr. Brunton; he rubbed his eyes, yawned and stretched. "I spoke to him first. My wife was still in bed, but I remembered him from a couple of days ago. He asked me if I'd seen a man with straw-coloured hair, name of McNab. I told him McNab was here the day before yesterday, but he left to look for his sister and her baby. He was hoping to find them alive here, and when he didn't he was at a loss, although he was interested in hearing about the sergeant who had saved the baby. He asked me where he should search for his sister, and I told him all the remains were being sent to Fortrose first, and then transported to Tararua Acre, and he could look there. He said that's where he would go, and he intended to stay there until he found her, one way or another. And that's what I told Smith. I suppose I shouldn't have, but he did have these two with him and they seemed to be real policemen."

"Even though they woke you in the middle of the night?"

A guilty expression flitted across William Brunton's face.

"We've been used to that this week. People have been arriving at all hours. So many people are looking for family who were on the *Tararua*, and I assumed the person knocking on the door was just one more person searching for a missing relative."

"When I came down, William was already sitting in the chair with a gun on him" said Mrs. Brunton. "Smith told these two to keep an eye on us until he got back, and then he went outside. I heard him taking a horse. I looked out the window as he left."

"Which one did he take, dear?" asked Mr. Brunton. "Not Nightingale, I hope."

"No. He took my show horse, the small bay with black points. It makes me think he isn't an experienced horseman. Nightingale would scare anyone who wasn't used to riding. She's a large horse, and fast. My horse is quite small and dainty, and not one most men find appealing."

"What about your son?" asked Frank. "Isn't he at home?"

Mrs. Brunton blushed and looked away.

"He spends the night in Fortrose sometimes." Mr. Brunton

sat up and squared his shoulders. "His wife died last year, and…"

"I understand," said Frank. "But the important thing is he wasn't at home. Probably just as well. He would have fought with them, and it could have ended much worse for you."

They nodded, cheered by the suggestion. Mrs. Brunton bit her lip, worrying about something. "Sergeant Hardy, Nightingale would be a perfect horse for you. I'd like you to have her. I like you, and I like your history. My husband doesn't ride any more, and the horse needs a big man who can handle her. Please take her with you now. You're going to need a horse. I'll send the papers to you care of the constabulary office in Wellington."

"As soon as we're done with all this, the burials, and the searches, and the inquest, we're going to the North Island to take the waters — to the hot springs at Lake Taupo." Mr. Brunton sighed. "I don't expect to return, not really, so I won't need a horse."

"Don't say that, my dearest." Mrs Brunton held her husband's hands in hers. "The hot springs have cured others. They'll fix you up as good as new. But I don't expect you'll ride again, and Charles has his own horse."

Inspector Buckley looked embarrassed at the display of affection. "We need to find Smith," he said. "But I can't leave the wreck site yet. Hardy, the best thing for you to do is to get away from here. Get your family down to Bluff and lock yourselves in a hotel. I'll be there as soon as I can. We'll keep an eye out for Smith as we search the beach."

He turned towards the sergeant and the constable. "I don't want to see your faces for a while. What I want you to do is go down to the shore and walk towards Porpoise Bay. Go along the water's edge as much as you can, and keep an eye open for any debris from the ship."

"Walk? But it's twenty miles to Porpoise Bay," protested the sergeant. "And what are we supposed to do when we get there?"

Inspector Buckley looked at him through narrowed eyes. "Turn around and come back."

"But…." The sergeant opened his mouth to protest, but the inspector stopped him with a raised hand.

"Consider yourselves lucky. You deserve to spend some time in the lockup, but I'm feeling generous. You're getting off lightly. Now, on your way."

The two men dragged themselves out the door, taking a last vengeful look at Frank.

Frank had been considering Mrs. Brunton's offer. He needed a new horse. His last one had died in his arms, and he'd been looking for another one that could become part of him in the way Copenhagen had. Nightingale fit the bill perfectly.

"I'd like to take the horse," he said. "But I'd have to pay you for her."

She shook her head. "We're handing the farm over to Charles," she said. "He has his own animals, and he doesn't want any of ours. William is very fond of Nightingale and would like to see her go to a nice family. My mind is made up. You must take Nightingale and I refuse to take any payment for her. It will cost to transport her back to Wellington, of course. And you can cover those expenses."

Frank and the inspector left Brunton Station and rode back to the beach astride Nightingale, who carried them both easily. Frank had forced six pounds onto Mrs. Brunton to pay for a saddle and bridle, and she'd taken it without argument, disappearing into the pantry to hide it somewhere. He hoped Mette still had some of her money left. They might find themselves begging for a place to sleep at the Bluff lockup if she didn't.

Mette jumped up from the tarpaulin when she saw them coming. Frank could see the relief in her eyes. She'd been given food and a blanket to wrap around herself and the girls, but she had been worried. He dismounted and nodded to Detective Tuohy, who had been left to stand guard. "Thank you, detective."

Inspector Buckley followed him, and crouched beside Mette. "You were right, Mrs. Hardy. Your husband has an excellent assistant for his detecting work. Mr. Smith was at Otara Station last night and took the Brunton's under his control. He left my two men — the two who were with you — to watch the family and came down here looking for somebody. You probably saved the Bruntons from considerable grief. And now I'm working on the premise that Smith murdered McNab."

He leaned over and tickled Helen, who giggled. "I have eight of these of my own," he said to Mette. "Six of them are girls. I miss them when I'm in the field."

"Eight children! How does your wife manage?"

"She has help." She saw a little smile cross his face. "I take the older ones to watch the cricket at the North Ground when I'm home. That way, she has a chance to rest. And the older girls mind the younger ones. You'll find that's how it works when you have a few more of your own."

Inspector Buckley sat down, stretching his legs. He moved

rather stiffly, and she wondered if he was feeling his age. He must be close to sixty.

"Now, I'd like to ask you a little more about Mr. Smith. When did you first see him, and what did you think of him?"

"Mr. Smith was on the train with me from Dunedin," she said. "And so was Mr. Hinton, Frank's gold robbery suspect. Actually, I thought Mr.Smith was following Mr. Hinton, but then I discovered he was following me, because I was carrying a baby. I first saw Mr. Smith on the train platform in Dunedin. He walked beside the train looking in the windows, and then jumped on board at the last minute — into my carriage. I thought he might be a policeman at first, and I guessed he was following someone. But I never dreamed it was me."

Inspector Buckley nodded. "He was looking for someone who looked like you, and he thought he'd found her." He leaned forward and massaged his calves. "I'd like to investigate the kidnapping further, especially Smith's part in it, but I have my work cut out for me here. We're charged with retrieving the mail bags and anything valuable — money, watches and such — that may have washed up from the wreck. I have men standing guard along the beach to prevent looting, not just of valuables, but also of small items that might be sold as relics in the future. I don't understand it myself, but people do it for the money. And we're still looking for bodies, of course."

"It's a terrible thing," she said. "All those poor people drowning like that. I feel so sad about it."

He patted her arm, then gestured to Detective Tuohy. "You and your husband need to go to Bluff and lock yourselves in a hotel. I'll send Detective Tuohy with you. You can take a cart into Fortrose and get the coach from there. Detective Tuohy will make sure you're alone in the coach. And of course your husband will ride beside the coach."

He turned to Frank. "Are you carrying a weapon, Sergeant?"

Frank shook his head.

"In that case, we'll get you one. Tuohy?"

The Detective hurried off to where a guard was watching the pack horses, and returned with a holstered gun and an ammunition pouch threaded onto a belt.

"An Adams Mark III revolver," said the inspector. "The same one the North-West Mounted Police have been using. You'll like it." He handed the gun to Frank. "Rather fancy joining them, myself, actually, up in the wilds of northern Canada, with a gold rush going on and all kinds of villains running around. I reckon they're like the Armed Constabulary were before the Police Act came into effect last year. More interesting than the work I'm doing now." He handed the gun and the ammunition pouch to Frank. "Ever used one of these?"

Frank took the gun from its holster and checked it out, spinning the barrel a couple of times. Spotless, of course, and well-oiled. "No. I have a Colt and an Enfield. I left them at home for this trip." He slid the cartouche box onto the belt and strapped the belt around his waist. "Should we be expecting an attack, do you think?"

"Best be safe," said the inspector. "Something is going on. We seem to have two separate crimes underway. I'm not counting out the gold robbery. Your man Hinton is still out there. You never know who might be coming after you. Get a room in a hotel — Scott's Club Hotel on the Bluff Parade is excellent. I'll be down as soon as I'm able to leave here."

14

The Coach to Bluff

The clerk at the post office in Fortrose grimaced as he dragged Mette's bag from the storeroom. "What are you carrying in this bag, Mrs. Hardy? A load of bricks?"

Mette, who had Sarah Jane strapped to her back again, took the Gladstone bag from him, smiling apologetically. "It's a manuscript. A very large manuscript that I'm going to have to translate when I get it home."

Frank moved Helen to his left side and took the bag from Mette. "Must be quite a manuscript. I wonder if Professor Mann knew how much it would weigh."

Mette sighed. "I think it's a thousand pages long. I read some of it, and it's really dull. I'm going to have an awful time earning my money."

"Talking of money, how much do you have left?"

She handed him the last of her bank notes, but kept a few coins. "Three pounds. Will that be enough to get us home? I have ten shillings in coins as well."

He shoved the money in his pocket. "Probably not. I'll have to find a way to get more. This should get us to Dunedin, and we'll worry about it then. I'll work on the docks if I have to."

She admired his ability to put off worrying. But he could go for days sleeping outside and not eating, whereas she needed a bed of some kind and at least two meals a day. The girls were an added problem, especially Helen, who was living on condensed milk and pap, which they would need to buy if they couldn't find a relative to care for her. Sarah Jane was no problem at all. Mette provided for all her needs.

Detective Tuohy was waiting outside with a Royal Mail coach and a uniformed coachman.

"This is Mr. O'Reilly." He nodded towards the coach driver, a sturdy man in his fifties who looked like he'd been born with a whip in his hand. "He's taking us directly to Bluff. He usually goes through Wyndham, but he's very kindly agreed to save us three hours."

"How much do we owe you?" asked Frank, putting his hand in his pocket. Not the pocket where he'd put Mette's three pounds, she noticed.

The detective waved him away. "The Invercargill Police are paying for it."

Frank grinned at Mette with one eyebrow raised.

Detective Tuohy put their bags on roof of the coach. "We have a long trip ahead of us, so make yourself comfortable," he said to Mette. "There's a basket of food for you, with some extra tins of condensed milk for the little one." He climbed up to the front seat and sat next to the coachman. She was to have the coach all to herself, her and the girls and a basket of food. How delightful!

The coach was very much like the one Frank had been driving when she first met him, and it brought back fond memories, as well as some rather frightening ones. She hoped the driver was as good as Frank, although they weren't going through the Manawatu Gorge this time, but across land that was quite flat, with occasional clumps of windblown trees, from what she remembered of her last trip in this direction.

Rain began as they left town, and a cold wind rattled the coach, creeping through the cracks in the doors. The road was un-metalled and rutted, and soon turned into a quagmire, slowing the coach to a crawl; Mette began to wonder if they would get to Bluff before nightfall. Frank had been following the coach on Nightingale; when it slowed down, he caught up and tapped on the window. She lowered it and leaned out, ignoring the rain, happy to see him again.

"I'm going on ahead to check the road. With this rain, we don't want any slips to catch us by surprise."

She was sure he must be thinking about the slip in the Seventy Mile Bush that had almost killed him, and the tree thrown across the road in the Gorge followed by the attack that Frank had just barely managed to stop. But he must not be enjoying the slow ride, now that he had a new horse. She suspected he was telling her he was looking for slips just so he could have a good gallop. She waved him away. "Off you go. We'll be alright."

To distract herself while he was gone, she opened the basket to see what Detective Tuohy had found for them. The basket was packed full. She moved everything around and discovered several tins of condensed milk for Helen, jars of potted meats, a tin of raspberry jam, some Canterbury cheese, bread, and a whole tin of biscuits. This trip was going to be nicer than she had imagined, in spite of the rain. She took out a digestive biscuit and broke off a crumb for Helen. She had intended to feed her some crumbs, like she did with Sarah Jane, but Helen grabbed the whole biscuit and crammed it into her mouth. When she realized that she couldn't swallow it all, her face fell and she tried to cry, her open mouth revealing the half-chewed biscuit.

Mette held her on her lap and removed as much of the biscuit as she could. Helen fought back vigorously, rearing back and clamping her mouth shut over Mette's probing finger.

"Now Helen," said Mette, releasing her hold on Helen's jaw. "You can't have all of it. You'll choke."

Helen's bottom lip came out and she started to sniff, dribbling chunks of biscuit down her chin.

Sarah Jane had been lying on the seat by Mette, wrapped in her blanket, half asleep. Helen's crying set her off as well. In a few minutes, they were both howling.

To make matters worse, the coach was swaying from side to side on the muddy road, reminding Mette of her trip by sea from Copenhagen. If it kept up she was going to vomit.

She unlatched the window of the coach and lowered it, looking out for Frank. The rain had stopped, but everything was wet, and the road was covered in puddles.

He was returning from his gallop and trotted up beside the coach. "Do you need something?"

Behind her, the cries had risen to a crescendo. He grinned down at her. "Can't you manage? Inspector Buckley's wife has eight like that."

"Not all this size," said Mette crossly. "I tried to stop Helen eating a whole biscuit because I was afraid she would choke, and that made her cry. Then Sarah Jane joined in. I don't know what I can do to quieten them. Could we get out and walk around for a bit? It feels cramped up in here."

"We're coming to the hill where we got you away from the sergeant and the constable," he said. "There's a ferry at the bottom. We'll be there in ten minutes. Can you wait until then?"

When she didn't reply, he said, "Why don't you hand Helen to me and I'll take her for a ride. We'll go down and look at the ferry."

"Are you sure? Isn't she too small to be taken on a horse?"

He leaned down and looked through the window. "Helen, do you want to come for a ride with Frank?"

She stopped screaming and gazed at him, tears still dribbling down her cheeks. "Fah?"

"Pass her through the window, Mette."

Mette complied, holding Helen tightly, worrying she would drop her, but almost feeling that it would serve her right if she did. But Frank managed to scoop her up and sat her on the saddle in front of him, held close enough to become part of him.

"Hang on, Helen." He took off at a trot, and Mette heard Helen squeal with delight. She turned to Sarah Jane and sighed. "Daddy will take you riding one day." Even a basket of food no longer cheered her up.

She picked up Sarah Jane and cuddled her. With Helen gone, Sarah Jane had quieted down and Mette thought they might both be able to sleep for a few minutes. Sarah Jane had her thumb in her mouth, and Mette removed it gently. She was determined not to have a child who sucked her thumb. She was drifting off when the coach lurched sideways suddenly, as if a wheel had come off. The coach righted itself and continued on, speeding up. She could see the trees flashing by on the side of the road, and spray kicking up from the puddles.

Something wasn't right. She put Sarah Jane on the floor of the coach to keep her secure and lowered the window to look for Frank. No sign of him, but the coachman's arm was hanging off the side, the reins still dangling from his fingers. He no longer had control of the coach. She heard Detective Tuohy yelling, but could not make out the words.

The coach continued to speed, and now they were at the hill. She moved Sarah Jane aside and lay beside her on the floor. Frank had once told her this was what she should do if she was ever in a runaway coach. The coach was swaying terribly, and her head kept knocking against the door.

They reached the trees where Frank had dropped onto the cart driven by the policemen. She half expected him to do it again, but of course he didn't. He was a mile away with Helen, unaware of what was happening to them.

After the coach passed the trees there was a long, slow curve. As they entered the curve, the coach slowly toppled over and landed on its side. The horses kept going, dragging it along that way for several minutes before coming to a stop. Her head hit against the door several times, but she had Sarah Jane in a tight hold. Nothing was going to hurt her.

When they came to a complete stop, she didn't move for several minutes. Then she opened Sarah Jane's blanket and ran her hands over her baby. Sarah Jane stared at her, thumb once more in her mouth. This time Mette left it there. "We're alright," she whispered. "We just had a nasty accident, but daddy will come and get us out."

As she spoke, she heard hoofbeats on the road. Someone jumped onto the side of the coach and opened the door above her head.

"Nice to see you again, Mrs. Hardy," said Roderick Smith.

* * *

She climbed out carrying Sarah Jane, refusing Mr. Smith's helping hand. Detective Tuohy was standing in front of the coach, nursing what looked like a broken right arm. The coachman lay at his feet, a pawing at a small red stain on the front of his shirt.

She stepped towards him. "Is he alright? Does he need help."

Detective Tuohy grimaced with pain. "Careful, Mrs. Hardy. He has a gun."

"Who…?"

She turned back to Mr. Smith. He had jumped down from the side of the coach and was holding a gun loosely by his side. Mrs. Brunton's horse was standing quietly beside the coach. A dainty bay, she had called it.

Mr. Smith gestured with his gun at Detective Tuohy. "You may as well help the coachman. I don't want another death on my conscience."

Mette took another step in the direction of the fallen coachman, looking desperately to see if Frank was coming around the curve.

"Not you, Mrs. Hardy. You stay where you are. I'm going to relieve you of your burden, if you don't mind."

"My burden?" She was puzzled. Did he want her Gladstone bag and the manuscript? Had that been what this was about all along?

"The child," he said. "Give me the child."

That was so ridiculous she almost laughed. "Why do you want my daughter?" she asked. "What possible reason could you have for taking my daughter?"

"She's not your daughter," he said confidently. "I…um… spoke to McNab last night, and he told me you and your husband have the child. I was following you and I saw your husband gallop away — I'm sure he'll be back in a minute. So I need you to give me the child before he returns."

"But he has…" she started to say. But how could she tell him there were two babies, and that he should wait until Frank returned to see the proof. He would shoot Frank and take Helen — perhaps even take both the girls. She had to persuade him that Sarah Jane was her own daughter.

Detective Tuohy was trying to stanch the flow of blood from the coachman's chest with his left hand. The coachman raised his head and said, "Sergeant Hardy has the child you're looking for. The baby with Mrs. Hardy is her own daughter. I saw them getting on to my coach."

"He's right," said Tuohy. His hand was pressed firmly on the coachman's chest, and he seemed to have stopped the flow of blood. "There are two babies. That one is the Hardy child."

Smith shook his head and sneered. "I suppose you think I should wait until Hardy returns. What kind of fool do you think I am, Tuohy?"

"I'm not giving you my baby," she said. "I'll die before I let you take my baby."

He aimed his gun at Detective Tuohy and said to Mette in a flat drawl, "No need for you to die, Mrs. Hardy. I dislike the idea of killing a woman. But if you don't hand me the baby immediately, I'll kill the detective. I'm sure your husband will be here in a minute and we don't have much time. What's it going to be? Should I kill Tuohy and take the baby, or should I just take the baby?"

She could feel a scream rising from her chest, but distantly, as if it came from someone else. She was reading this in a book, or watching it in a play, and saying to the character that was herself, "Don't do it, don't do it."

He backed over to her and put his arm around Sarah Jane. "Here you are young lady. Let's get you back to your father."

Mette was frozen with horror. "No, please. Don't take her."

He tore Sarah Jane from her, his gun still trained on Detective Tuohy. "Let her go," said the detective in a flat voice. "Your husband will find him and kill him. He'll get your baby back."

Mr. Smith put his foot in the stirrup and jumped nimbly onto the horse, holding Sarah Jane tightly to him. Her mind, still hovering somewhere above her head, said, he can ride. Mrs. Brunton was wrong. But it's such a small horse and Frank will be able to ride him down. But the part of her mind that still resided in her head said, and then what?

And then he was off, heading through the trees and towards the river.

Mette dropped to her knees and doubled over, unable to breath, gasping for air. She thought she had never felt such pain in her whole life.

She was still like that when Frank returned five minutes later. He trotted around the curve holding Helen, saw the terrible tableau vivant, and broke into a canter for the last few hundred yards.

"What happened here? Is everyone alright?"

"He took the baby. Mr. Smith took our Sarah Jane. He thought she was Helen."

Frank bent down from the saddle and thrust Helen into Mette's arms.

"Which way did he go?" he asked Tuohy. His voice sounded harsh.

"He took the bridle path towards the river." Tuohy pointed with his uninjured arm towards the trees. "He has about five minutes start, but he's on a small horse. You'll catch him if you go straight back down to the river."

Frank pulled on Nightingale's reins and turned her around. Mette thought she had never seen his face so dark and determined.

"It'll be slow going for him on the bridle path," said Tuohy. "He'll be trying for the ferry, or the river mouth. But the river mouth is tidal and broad. He'll sink into the sand if he tries to cross."

Frank nodded his thanks to Tuohy, and spurred Nightingale back the way he had just come; he turned first, his face dark with rage, his voice harsh. "Don't move from here until I get back. I'll send help as soon as I find Smith and get my daughter back."

And with that, he thundered away on his pale grey horse, both of them looking like death.

Mette had still not quite grasped what had happened. She plunked Helen down beside the detective and strode over to the coach. "I'll get a napkin to help stop the bleeding."

She climbed onto the side of the coach and opened the door upwards. If she lay flat, she could just reach the Gladstone bag, and she knew she had left a couple of extra napkins inside, wrapped around the manuscript. It seemed extra heavy, but she dragged it out and slid off the coach. Then she snapped open the bag and reached in.

Nothing.

She had the wrong bag.

151

She had picked up the bag of that bloody red-haired American.

Everything hit her at once.

Her daughter had been taken.

Frank was chasing the terrible man who had taken her, but the countryside was wild and unfamiliar to Frank. He wouldn't know where Smith might be going, in spite of what the detective had told him.

And now, on top of everything else, she had the wrong bag.

She bent over in terrible grief, pounding on the bag, unable to breath, trying to scream.

"My baby. My baby."

15

The Chase

The drumbeat of Nightingale's hooves played the words of *The Charge of the Light Brigade* in Frank's head. *Half a league, half a league, half a league, onward.* It was echoed by the pounding of his heart in his chest. He could scarcely recognize his own emotions. He'd fought in wars and seen terrible things; he'd lost his own brother to a brutal enemy act. But nothing had prepared him for how he might feel if he lost his beloved daughter.

The horse took the road at a gallop, flying along the rutted surface like a thoroughbred on a race course. The bridle path appeared through the trees briefly, and he realized that it split in two, with one part going towards the ocean, the other continuing down to the river. If Smith had gone in the direction of the ocean he could turn inland anywhere and be impossible to find. He had to believe he'd gone to the ferry, knowing that crossing the river would give him an unbeatable head start. He'd seen the empty punt pulling in when he was at the ferry with Helen, twenty minutes ago. The ferrymen had told him the punt would depart for the far side as soon as they had a passenger. If he could get there before the punt pulled out he could stop Smith and rescue Sarah Jane.

He was at the river in ten minutes, in time to see the ferry punt pulling out into the stream, swaying as the current tried to push it off its cables and downstream towards the ocean. He could see Smith in the centre, facing the far side, holding onto the horse with one hand, Sarah Jane tucked under his arm. He was the only passenger on board; a pole-man stood at the front of the punt making sure it didn't snag on anything. On the far side, a coach awaited, ready for the return trip. That would slow things down, especially if Smith didn't see him coming.

He checked his belt for the gun Inspector Buckley had lent him. It was loaded and ready to go, but how could he shoot at Smith, knowing he was carrying Sarah Jane? He had always been a dead shot who hardly ever missed his target. But he'd never had to shoot a man who was carrying his own child. A bullet did not know enough to stop when it entered one body. It could just as easily continue on into another body. Chances were he would not be able to use the gun.

"Is there any other way to get across the river so I can meet the ferry?" he asked the cable operators. They were sweating over the handles of the cable wheel and took a moment to answer, then both looked up at him.

"There's a bridge…ten miles…to the east," one said between grunts.

"Too far." The other man stopped pushing the wheel, but left his hands in place, ready to continue. "Take the path along the river towards the ocean and cross where it curves back away from Fortrose. It's shallow there. Then go along the beach for a bit and turn inland."

They returned to their labours. As he spurred his horse towards the coast, he heard one say, "Bad idea. The river is sandy near the mouth and it's treacherous."

He was at the curve in minutes, and forced the horse into the shallow water. Nightingale moved carefully, testing the firmness of the sand. He leaned over and watched the water in front of him, searching for small disturbances in the water that indicated drops in the riverbed, stroking the horse's mane, to calm himself, but also because he needed both of them to get across the river. "Careful now, Nightingale."

At the mid-point, he came upon a shoal; it was below the surface, and the horse stopped, refusing to move forward. He dismounted and led her, making sure there were no holes she could step into, feeling in front of himself with one foot before putting his full weight on the stony shoal.

Less than five yards from the bank on the far side, he felt firm sand. The current was stronger as the water concentrated into a race, pulling at his legs, and he held on to Nightingale's saddle and let her take him the last part of the way. In spite of its firmness, the sand kept dissolving under his feet, but they made it to the edge and struggled together up onto the bank.

Astride the horse once more, he hurtled along the beach for two hundred yards and then headed inland again until he met the river, where a decent track had been constructed; he followed it towards the ferry, letting the horse have her head, calculating when the ferry punt would dock on this side of the river. He should arrive at the same time as the punt, or soon after. And it would take time for the poleman to secure the boat to the dock. No one would be allowed to disembark until that job was complete.

The punt was already docking when he arrived. The poleman carried the rope wound around his arm ready to tie it to the cleat. Smith hadn't seen Frank coming, and stood at the front of the punt, ready to disembark, still holding the horse and Sarah Jane.

When he saw Frank approaching along the path, he took a step back and said to the poleman, "I've changed my mind. I'd like to return to the other side, if you please. Push off."

"Not so quick, sir," said the poleman. "I always have a pipe before I cross back. I'll leave in ten minutes."

Smith let go of the horse and retreated to the rear of the punt, clutching Sarah Jane.

Frank jumped from Nightingale and waded out into the waist-deep water. "Give me my daughter, Smith."

"Push off, push off," Smith looked around frantically. "This man is a kidnapper. I'm a police officer, and I just rescued the baby from his wife. They're both criminals."

"He's no police officer." Frank plunged into the water, grabbed the side of the punt and hoisted himself on board. "He stole my daughter. You're finished, Smith. Give Sarah Jane to me."

Smith pulled out his gun. "Get off the punt, now, or I'll shoot."

Frank could see the gun hadn't been cocked, and he hit Smith hard on his wrist with both fists, coming from below. The gun flew from Smith's hand and into the water, bouncing along the surface like a stone tossed by a schoolboy. Frank reached for Sarah Jane, who was staring at him trustingly. She raised her arms towards him and chuckled.

Before he could grab her, the poleman stepped between them and took her from Smith. "I don't know who this baby belongs to, but I'm going to keep her until someone I'm sure is from the police tells me the truth."

"You can ask Inspector Buckley, from the Invercargill police" said Frank. He could feel his body tingling with relief. "Or Mr. and Mrs. Brunton from Otara station. They both know Smith was there and that he killed a man."

The poleman looked from one to the other, wavering.

"Is there a problem here?" asked someone from the bank of the river.

A coach had arrived at the dock and disgorged a well-dressed couple, the man with a distinct military bearing. They were standing at the end of the dock, flanked by two sturdy coachmen, watching the action with interest. Frank recognized the man's suit as one he'd seen at Te Aro House: a Mosgiel Tweed. He took a second to admire the cut, and the way it hung from the man's shoulders, and then turned back to Smith, seized him by the scruff of his neck and pulled him up onto his toes against the railing.

Smith was surprisingly calm, sneering at Frank as if he were still in control of the situation. "I'm a policeman," he said loudly. "I'm from the Dunedin station. I'm trying to arrest this man for kidnapping." He stamped on Frank's foot, causing Frank to loosen his hold on the collar, and jumped away. Frank followed him as he backed along the rail and into the corner of the punt. He put his fists up at Frank and said, "I was on the boxing team at Dunedin Boys High School. I dare you to make a move. I'm arresting you for kidnapping, and murder. Anything you say…"

Frank pulled back his fist and slammed it into Smith's nose, where it landed with a satisfying crunch. Smith crumpled to the ground, a look of astonishment on his face, blood pouring from his nostrils.

"And I was the regimental champ," said Frank. "Stand up and I'll hit you again."

"Could someone tell me what is going on here?" asked the older man on the dock.

The poleman turned towards him and gestured at Frank and Smith. "We have someone here claiming to be a policeman, and he's trying to arrest this tall bloke who just hit him for trying to take his baby away. I don't know who's telling the truth, sir. But I saw the tall bloke with a baby earlier on. He came down to the ferry when we were on the other side and he asked when we were leaving."

Frank massaged his knuckles, relieved that the poleman couldn't tell one baby from another.

The man from the coach surveyed them thoughtfully. "Well, I'm a magistrate. And I'd like to hear what each of you has to say."

The woman beside him spoke up quietly. "That baby is the image of the tall gentleman. How could anyone doubt that she belongs to him?"

The magistrate glanced at his wife and nodded. Frank half expected he would, Solomon-like, offer to cut the baby in half. He was elated, knowing that he had his Sarah Jane back. No one was taking her away from him now. He would fight them all if he had to.

"Can you tell me anything about this child that would convince me she is yours?" said the magistrate to Frank.

Frank thought for a minute. What did he know about Sarah Jane that distinguished her from all the other six-month-old babies in the world? Then he remembered her birth, during the flood, and how he had cut the umbilical cord with his own knife. "She has a tummy button that sticks out in an odd way," he said. "I was there when she was born, and I had to tie the knot in the cord."

The poleman opened Sarah Janes' dress. "It certainly does stick out," he said. "I've never seen one like that before."

The magistrate stepped onto the punt, holding the railing to keep his balance, and checked Sarah Jane. He smiled and nodded at Frank. "You're right. I haven't seen one like that before either. She's going to have to explain it to her husband one day." He took Sarah Jane in his arms and looked down at her. "You have an adorable daughter, Mr….what did you say your name was?"

"Hardy," said Frank. "Sergeant Frank Hardy."

"Of the 57th Regiment?" asked the magistrate. "A Die hard? I remember reading about you in dispatches. Quite often, I seem to recall. I was a colonel in the 57th., back in the days of the Taranaki Wars. Regimental boxing champion, you say?"

Frank nodded, although it wasn't exactly true. He'd thrashed the regimental champion once, if that counted. He was itching to take back Sarah Jane, but this was not the time to rush things.

Roderick Smith, who had clambered to his feet and was trying to stop the flow of blood from his damaged nose, seemed to realize that things weren't going his way. He took off his coat and threw it at Frank and then vaulted over the railing of the punt into the river, landing up to his chest in water beside the dock. Then he dived in and struck out towards the opposite bank, swimming strongly. About ten yards out, the current picked him up and pulled him downstream. He stayed afloat, flailing madly, trying to swim towards the other side, but the current got to better of him. As they watched, he was taken downstream, bobbing fruitlessly in the racing water.

159

Frank had thrown Smith's coat down and lunged for him, but everything had happened too fast. He watched Smith disappear downstream, knowing he wasn't going to follow him into the water. Not with Sarah Jane rescued and waiting to be returned to her mother. Smith could save himself.

"I'd like to go after him." The poleman shrugged apologetically. "But I can't swim. He'll be alright, won't he?"

The magistrate shaded his eyes with one hand and scanned the surface of the river. "He may make it," he said. "Foolish chap, jumping into the water like that. What was he trying to get away from?"

"Hanging," said Frank. "We can't convict him without a trial, but I believe he killed a man. The man who kidnapped the other baby girl."

"There are two?" asked the magistrate. "Interesting. Are you intending to cross the river? Perhaps you'd be so kind as to tell me all about it as we cross?"

The poleman sat on the bench on the dock and smoked his pipe while the two coachmen manoeuvred the coach onto the punt and pulled the brakes into place, setting chocks by the wheels to be extra sure it would stay still. Frank had done that himself once, and he appreciated the extra effort.

After some jockeying, they decided they would have to make two trips. The magistrate's wife would go first in the coach with the two coachmen, and Frank, the magistrate, and the horses would follow on a second trip.

When everything was in place and the brake applied to the wheels of the coach, the poleman signalled the two men on the other side; they were going to have their work cut out for them, pulling such a heavy load, even without Frank and the horses on board. However, once the punt began moving along the chains, the movement of the river helped. The poleman was straining on his pole at the rear of the punt, doing what he could to help the other two.

The punt returned and Frank and the magistrate climbed aboard. Frank tied the two horses to the rails and leaned beside them holding Sarah Jane close to his heart, trying not to grin. He was already imagining Mette's reaction when he returned to the mail coach with Sarah Jane. More than anything, he wanted to see her face when he trotted around the bend carrying Sarah Jane in his arms.

When she saw him coming, she rose from the spot where she had been sitting on the side of the road, and looked in his direction, her hands over her mouth. He knew she must be terrified about what he was bringing back, and so he waved at her to let her know he had a living baby in his arms, and she ran towards him. Afraid to scare Sarah Jane, he slowed Nightingale to a slow trot, smiling and enjoying the moment. They met fifty yards from the coach and he jumped down and handed Sarah Jane to her. Then he wrapped both of them in his arms and stood there holding each other. He felt better than he had in his entire life.

A little voice said, "Fah?"

Helen had crawled out into the road and was clutching at Frank's trouser leg. He knew she needed attention, but this was Sarah Jane's moment. He picked her up and carried her back to where Detective Tuohy sat and plunked her down. "Could you watch this one for a few minutes, Tuohy?"

He would sort everything out eventually, but he wasn't finished enjoying his moment yet.

16

The Bottom of the Bag

Now that she had Sarah Jane back, all Mette wanted was to get to a hotel in Bluff and pop the two girls into a warm bath. Their clothes were grubby and their napkins needed changing. She had no spare ones with her because of the Gladstone bag mistake, and the best she could do was to rinse the ones they were wearing in a puddle and wring them out as hard as she could. The girls both resisted having a damp napkin wrapped around them and held in place with a pilch, but there was no choice; she could hardly leave their bottoms bare. Once their own little bodies warmed up the wetness, they settled down and accepted the change.

How stupid of her to pick up the wrong bag in Wyndham. She was certainly not going to tell Frank what she had done. Not yet. He needn't know that the manuscript, one of their best chances for making money, was gone. She would tell him when they were on the way home, when everything was back to normal.

She imagined the red-haired American opening the bag when he reached Melbourne and discovering a boring thousand page book. Of course, there was nothing in his bag, so he must be planning to pick up some gold along the way, probably somewhere in Bluff, and he would discover the mistake then. He would toss out the manuscript, or burn it, and use the spare napkins as towels, not knowing what their real purpose was. Professor Mann was sure to be upset, but with all that had happened, how he felt was the least of her problems. Perhaps she wouldn't tell him it was lost, either. She would think of a story to tell him later.

Once Frank returned with Sarah Jane, everything had happened in a blur of love and action. The older couple who had come from the ferry with Frank — colonel something or other and his wife — had offered to take the wounded coachman to Fortrose, and had left one of their own coachmen to drive Mette and the girls to Bluff. Detective Tuohy had gone back to Fortrose with Mrs. Brunton's bay, hoping to ingratiate himself with the family, she imagined.

As soon as the men had managed to push the coach upright, she had climbed on board with the babies. Frank rode beside them on Nightingale, vowing not to budge an inch away for any reason. She felt very safe, even when they crossed the river and found the poleman staring downstream through a telescope, searching for Smith.

"No sight of him," he said. "Could have been thrown ashore at the bend. But I doubt he'll come back. Probably half way to the West Coast by now with a different name and a gold mining licence."

"I'll keep an eye open for him," Frank said. "He may still come after me. When we get to the Bluff we'll stay locked in the hotel until we hear from Inspector Buckley. Tuohy will

163

tell Buckley the whole story and he'll put the word out. They'll know about him, even on the West Coast. He won't get away."

Finally, after what seemed like hours of bumping along the road, they arrived in Bluff, the coach pulling up at Scott's Club Hotel on Gore Street, opposite the port. She caught glimpses of the ocean through the window of the coach, and hoped that meant they would have a view of the harbour from their room. She loved a nice view. The water looked calm compared to what she'd seen in Fortrose; she could see a ship entering the harbour, sails down, ready to dock at the wharf beyond the railway station.

"This is more like it." Frank grinned. "A decent hotel with private apartments and a billiard room, right across from the train station. A good dining room as well. No need to leave the premises for any reason. I'll have to send a telegram to Colonel Roberts and tell him what happened. At least he can let the Melbourne Constabulary know that Hinton might be returning there, and that Sampson tried to tell me he knew where the gold was. But that can wait until Inspector Buckley gets here. I'll talk it over with him."

She noticed that the hotel had a sign in the entrance saying there was a bathing room with hot and cold baths, which would be nice, especially if bathing was included in the room price. And private apartments. She hoped three pounds and ten shillings was going to be enough to pay for this luxury. She and Frank would have to go down to the baths one at a time, however. She refused to leave Sarah Jane alone ever again until she was grown up. Looking back, she was shocked with herself for leaving her alone in Dunedin when she went to collect the manuscript.

The owner of the hotel, Captain Scott, came out to meet them, directing Frank to the stables next to the hotel. He acted as if he had been expecting them, and she wondered if Inspector Buckley had contacted him. The inspector had mentioned this hotel as one they should stay at, because it was run by an ex-military man. Military men watched each other's backs, in her experience.

"I'll be in the stables next door for a while," Frank said to her. "I need to brush the horse down and made sure she's fed and watered. She's a fine horse and she's going to suit me very well." He patted the horse on her long, powerful neck and turned back to Mette. "Don't open the door to anyone, whatever you do. No one but me. I'll be back soon, I promise."

"If you would follow me, Mrs. Hardy," said Captain Scott. "I'll show you to your apartment."

The apartment had a bedroom with a bed and a cot, and a sitting room with a large wardrobe with a mirror on the door. It had been ages since she'd seen herself in a mirror, especially a full-sized mirror. When Captain Scott left she would have a good look at herself from all angles. She wanted to look older and more sophisticated, more of a woman of the world, so people wouldn't think she was Frank's daughter.

"Is there anything I can send up for you, Mrs. Hardy?" Captain Scott asked. "We have some fresh oysters, caught this morning. Perhaps a plate of those with some lemon and a few water biscuits?"

She was tempted. "That does sound delicious," she said. "But perhaps I'll wait until my husband is finished with his horse." And I'll ask him if we can even afford a plate of Bluff Oysters, she thought but didn't say. "Could someone bring me a bathing tub with warm water for the babies?"

"Certainly," he said. "I'll have the girl bring it up for you. And some soap as well. Perhaps you and your husband would like to take a bath in the bathing rooms later? We have hot and cold baths, and a salt water bath as well. Very private if you want to bathe together."

She agreed that perhaps they might, but knew she was never going to leave Sarah Jane by herself ever again. In fact, Frank could have a bath if he wished and she would do what she could with the babies' bath water.

She had bathed and fed the girls and tucked them into bed, and was soaking her feet in the still warm water, when she heard a knock on the door.

She dried her feet and went to the door, remembering Frank's instructions, afraid to open it but too curious not to find out who it was. The knock came again, soft and insistent. "Can I help you?" she asked, worried. What if it was Mr. Smith, come to find her again? She couldn't face another ordeal like that.

"Telegram for Sergeant Frank Hardy," said a youthful voice on the other side of the door. "Captain Scott said I could come up."

She opened the door part way, leaving the chain on, and peered through the crack. A young man in a telegraph cap was standing outside holding an envelope in his hand.

"Sergeant Hardy is in the stables next door to the hotel," she said, then wished she hadn't alerted him to the fact that she was alone. She should have said her husband was asleep in the sitting room.

"If you're his wife, I can give it to you."

The desire to know what was in the telegram overwhelmed

her. She had never been able to wait for news or for any kind of surprise. She reached through the gap in the door and took the telegram and then pulled her hand back quickly. He waited, smiling.

It took her a minute to understand why he wasn't moving, but when she did she reached into her pocket and found a penny, probably her last one, and handed it to him.

"Thanks, missus." He touched his cap and walked quickly down the hallway to the stairs. Apparently a penny was sufficient. Frank would have given him at least thruppence, but the young man didn't know that.

She tore open the envelope, worried now. She had never received a telegram herself, but knew they contained bad news as much as they contained good news. What if someone had died?

She saw to her relief that the telegram was from Colonel Roberts, the officer who had sent Frank south to follow the gold robbers:

> *Apologies for sending you into a disaster. Stop. Rooms reserved and paid for at Scott's Club Hotel, Bluff. Stop. Constabulary will cover return trip by rail or sea and all expenses for you and family. Stop. Kind Regards. Colonel James Roberts. Wellington Constabulary.*

No wonder Captain Scott seemed to have been expecting them. The bill had already been paid. Would that include food? She read the telegram again. It did say *"All* expenses." She was sure Frank would assume the expenses included a plate of Bluff oysters and a pint or two of beer. If she ignored the arrest and the sinking ship, this would end up being a very nice holiday, even if they didn't make any money. She decided she would try to be like Frank for a while and look on the bright side of things.

Sarah Jane started whimpering again, and she went over to the cot to check her. She had made a nest for the girls using bags and blankets so they wouldn't roll out of bed, but Helen was taking up most of the room, and had kicked the blankets off both of them. In spite of her ever-so-slight dislike of Helen, she had to admit she was an active child, advanced for her age if she was as young as she looked, and with lots of gumption. No wonder Frank was drawn to her. She sat on the edge of the cot and eased the two apart, trying not to wake them.

They rolled back together immediately, Helen with her arm slung casually over Sarah Jane's face. Sarah Jane's eyes fluttered, which happened when she was about to wake up.

Perhaps for the night, Captain Scott would bring up another bed. But for now it would be best if she moved Sarah Jane to the middle of the larger bed, where was she likely to stay in one place, and give Helen free rein of the cot.

Pushing the Gladstone bag to one side, she lifted Sarah Jane from the bed. She was about to put her on the large bed when the bag fell to the floor with a loud thump. She finished settling Sarah Jane and picked up the bag, wondering again why it weighed so much. It was empty, and it was the same as the bag she had been carrying, which was heavy, but not nearly as heavy as this one.

She sat on the floor beside the bag and opened it, feeling around inside to see if there was something in it that she hadn't noticed — a rock or a slab of granite, perhaps. She could feel nothing, but she noticed her hand did not seem to go as deep as it did with her own bag. She picked up the bag with her hand sill inside, and measured it with her eye. No, there was something on the bottom. In fact, it almost seemed as if it had a false bottom.

She dragged the bag nearer to the window where the light was better and opened it as wide as it would go. Then she ran her fingers across the bottom, looking to see if she could find a place to pry it away from the outer part of the bag. Nothing. It was glued in solidly, but she felt a bump at one end. By moving it around more she found a little notch with something she recognized: a tiny keyhole! She had been right: a false bottom.

She searched the room for something she could use to break open the bag. Nothing there, so she checked the girls to make sure they were secure, and went to into the sitting room. It was a small room with a single sofa in front of a fireplace and a table with a lamp. On the hearth, a set of fire irons hung from a cast iron frame. She picked up the poker, but it was too blunt. The slice bar next to it looked better, with its flat end. She took that and returned to the bedroom.

She could not move the bottom of the bag from its false bottom, but managed to pry it open a tiny bit. When she held the bag up to the window, something gleamed through the opening. It looked like gold. She sat back, thrilled. Had she accidentally taken the bag of a gold thief? Would that mean they would be able to claim the reward? She couldn't wait until Frank returned from the stable. He would be able to pry it open. Perhaps, finally, all their money problems were over. They could claim the reward.

She stood at the window, quivering with excitement, waiting for Frank, and saw him entering the shipping office. After ten minutes he came out again and hurried towards the wharf.

What was he up to? Had he seen someone? Perhaps Mr. Smith had found them. That thought dampened her excitement, and she went to the door to make sure it was locked. She checked the weight of the wardrobe to see if she could drag it across in front of the door, but was unable to move it. Instead, she set the heavy Gladstone bag against the door. It wouldn't help much, but if anyone tried to open the door she would lean against it and scream her head off.

17

The Red-Haired American

Frank had pried several small stones out of Nightingale's hooves and was grooming her with a bristle brush while she ate her oats, when he saw someone he thought he recognized come out of the shipping office across the street and head towards the wharf. He put down the brush and and stood in the shadows, checking to see if he'd been right.

Robert Hinton, his red hair bright in the pale sunlight, had come out of the shipping office across the road and was walking quickly towards the wharf, his Gladstone bag in one hand and a duffle bag over his shoulder. He had the sprightly walk of someone who thought he had got away with something.

Frank had promised Mette he'd be with her as soon as he was done with Nightingale. But the opportunity facing him was much too tempting to ignore; if he caught the last of the robbers carrying gold ingots, he could claim the reward and they'd be set for life.

He considered running up to tell Mette first, but if for some reason they knew nothing at the shipping office it would be too late to catch Hinton. No, for once he was going to have to break his word. He'd start at the shipping office in hopes of getting a quick answer and then search the wharf. The post office was beside the train station, and he could send a telegram to Colonel Roberts later, after he'd checked to make sure Mette was safe.

He pulled Nightingale into a stall, took off her feed bag, and hurried across the road. If the authorities in Melbourne heard Hinton was on his way there, and that he might be carrying stolen gold, they would search him when he disembarked. No need to leave Mette by herself for long. He'd be back in a minute.

But the shipping office was crowded with people queuing for tickets, with only one harried clerk manning the desk.

A fashionably-dressed young man at the back of the queue took his pocket watch from his waistcoat pocket and shook his head at Frank. "Don't bother waiting," he said. "I've been here for almost an hour. He's painfully slow. He's served just three people since I arrived. I'd leave if I thought I could come back later and find the place empty, but I suspect it'll be the same tomorrow. The *Tararua* sinking has created a backlog of passengers wanting to get to Port Phillip and Melbourne."

"Did you happen to notice a man with red hair?" asked Frank. "I saw him leave here a few minutes ago."

"The American?" He returned his watch to his waistcoat pocket and adjusted the chain so it hung correctly. "He was in front of me in the queue for a few minutes, then he left. He said he didn't want to wait around, and that he'd buy his ticket on board from the purser. That's all very well if you're travelling steerage, but I want a decent berth. I like to travel in comfort. I'm staying right here until the clerk can attend to me personally."

"Did the American happen to say which ship he was taking?"

The young man shook his head. "He didn't. But I saw three steamers at anchor in the harbour as I came from my hotel. I'm buying a ticket on one of them — the *Hawea* which docks in the morning. I'll still be in the queue when it sails, at this rate."

"Is the *Hawea* going to Melbourne?"

"Not immediately. It's heading back to Lyttelton first. But one of the other two steamers out there will be going to Melbourne, I imagine. Check the *Southland Times*. They always have the shipping arrivals and departures on the front page."

Frank thanked him and left, hoping it wasn't too late to catch Hinton. He crossed the train tracks and went down to the wharf, sure Hinton was planning to catch a steamer going to Melbourne, and soon.

The street at the entrance to the wharf was lined with shipping agents, a custom shed, a shed housing the tide gauge, and a watersiders' canteen. He scanned the interior of the canteen in case Hinton was inside, and then walked quickly onto the wharf. If Hinton was here he had him cornered.

The wharf ran out into the harbour for a hundred feet and then split into two parts. To the right, a short extension curved around a basin where fishing boats bobbed at anchor. A fishing boat was unloading a fresh catch of tuna and snapper, while an oyster dredge piled high with Bluff oysters waited to dock. Neither boat had enough space for a passenger, even if there was somewhere they could take Hinton, who would be looking for a ship headed out into international waters, probably on its way to Australia, and leaving soon.

The left arm of the wharf was longer — a good half mile

— and crowded with men going about their business: clerks gathered outside a customs shed holding shipping manifests, wharfies laboured to load several ships docked along the wharf, and porters pushed trolleys loaded with boxes towards the customs shed. None of the ships were passenger ships, which would anchor out in the harbour until it was time to collect passengers.

Tenders were occasionally to transport passengers out to a ship, or to bring them in, but most of the time, boarding was by gangplank from the wharf, as it had been with the *Tararua* in Wellington.

He walked along the wharf, checking the names of the ships and memorizing them. About half way along, two ships were being loaded with bales for transportation to England. Hinton could have found himself a berth on a wool ship. He could even have found a job on one. But he'd been queuing for a passenger ticket and intended to buy it onboard the ship from the purser. No, he was on his way out to a passenger steamer.

He searched the harbour for tenders. There were two, one coming in from the direction of the heads, and one leaving. The departing tender was a hundred yards out, with two crewmen rowing in unison and a passenger seated at the stern. He was almost positive that the passenger was Hinton. He squinted at the tender, watching to see where it went, and hoping he'd find someone to tell him the name.

As he watched, the tender was swallowed up by a swarm of small boats, many of them manned by Maori. Something unusual was going on out there. As a whaling port in the early nineteen hundreds, Bluff had seen many marriages between Maori woman and European whalers and their descendants still filled the town.

He walked up and down the wharf, wondering if he should send a telegram to Colonel Roberts anyway, and tell him a ship might be heading for Melbourne with Hinton, and that he might have the gold with him. But that was foolish. Too many might's, as it stood. Someone here must know more. If he knew where each of the steamers was headed, he could send a telegram to Colonel Roberts confident that one of the ships leaving for Australia today would be carrying Hinton and his gold. He already knew the *Hawea* was headed to Lyttelton.

The second tender he had glimpsed separated itself from the mass of small boats, and headed towards the landing; one lone man sat in the prow, his hand trailing in the water, while two crewmen pulled on the oars behind him. Frank waited for the men to tie the boat up and called down to them, "What ship have you come from?"

The man in the prow hopped onto the landing and mounted the ladder looking up at Frank. "The *Rotomahana*. We arrived from Melbourne an hour ago."

"When's the ship leaving?"

"Tomorrow, first tide. On its way north."

"Did someone just come out to the ship in a tender?"

The man shook his head. "I didn't see anyone. This is the only tender belonging to the *Rotomahana*." He stepped off the ladder, and tripped, but righted himself quickly. He was a tall, dark-haired man, about Frank's height, but younger and thinner, with the flushed face of a drinker and the long, thin nose of an aristocrat. "They're boarding tomorrow, as soon as the sun's up." As he passed Frank, he gave off a strong smell of whisky. He walked away, staggering slightly, and reached into his pocket, withdrawing a metal flask. He took a long swig, turned, and grinned at Frank. "My word, there are a lot of

175

boats in the harbour today. Is that a normal state of affairs?"

Frank ignored him. One of the ships in the harbour had raised its anchor and was belching steam from its stacks, signalling its departure.

"Do you know the name of that ship?" he asked a wharfie leaning on the ladder to the landing puffing on a pipe. "The one that's leaving?"

The wharfie glanced idly in the direction Frank was pointing and shrugged. "Dunno."

"Does anyone know?"

"The *Hawea*?" guessed a grey-bearded man sitting on a capstone nearby staring at nothing. "Or the *Rotomahana*? Maybe the *Te Anau*? They're all due this week."

"The *Hawea* isn't leaving until tomorrow. And the *Rotomahana* just got in."

He couldn't decide what he should do. He could find the newspaper and see what ships were due to leave and then telegraph Colonel Roberts. But what if Hinton was heading back to America? On the very ship Frank could see leaving? Maybe he was on his way to Port Arthur in Tasmania, or Sydney, rather than Melbourne? No, he needed to know what ship Hinton had boarded and where it was going. The *Te Anau* seemed to be the best possibility, but he had to be sure.

He worried for a moment about Mette, alone in the room with the girls and decided he had to take the chance and find where Hinton had gone. Mette would be alright for a bit longer. And the reward for finding out who had taken the gold was important for their future.

"Is there a place where I can see a ship up close as it leaves the harbour?" he asked the wharfie.

"Try the pilot station at Stirling Point." The wharfie emptied his nose off the side of the wharf and wiped his hand on his trousers. "The boats go real close to the point. The pilot keeps his cutter there, and there's a light. Don't want ships running up on the coast, like the *Tararua*. Did you hear about the *Tararua*?"

Frank raced back to the stable and threw his saddle back on Nightingale. He'd be back in no time. Mette would understand, once he told her why he'd left. The possibility of making a thousand pounds was churning in his head. What a boost that would be to their finances. It would solve everything.

Stirling Point was a mile or more away from the port, along a dirt track, nestled beneath The Bluff, the hill for which the town was named. He was there in less than ten minutes. The pilot was in his cutter, with two men pushing it out.

"Are you off to meet a ship?" he asked.

The pilot put his hand to his ear, signalling he hadn't heard.

"He's meeting the *Te Anau*, to guide it around the coast and past Dog Island," said one of men helping the pilot. "It's on the way to Melbourne, stopping at Port Phillip in Tasmania first."

The *Te Anau*, then. He looked at the pilot station and saw that a short ladder ran up one side to the lamp. "Do you mind if I climb up the station to take a look at the ship as it passes?"

The pilot didn't answer, and the man who had answered him shrugged. Taking that for permission, he climbed the ladder and clung to the top. The wind buffeted him, but he could see the *Te Anau* coming. He watched, hoping he'd see some final proof.

It took another twenty minutes, but the ship came right at him, less than five hundred yards away. The pilot's cutter went out to meet it, and the pilot was pulled on board. He shook someone's hand — the captain, Frank assumed — and headed to the wheelhouse.

He scanned the ship, looking for Hinton, thinking it would be a miracle if he found him. But standing at the prow, his duffle bag and his Gladstone bag on the deck beside him, there he was. Robert Hinton, on his way to Melbourne with the gold. Success!

Frank slid down the ladder and vaulted back onto Nightingale. He raced back into Bluff feeling absurdly happy, dying to tell Mette that he had secured the reward and their future.

Mette could wait a few more minutes, however. First, he had to send a telegram to Colonel Roberts, informing him that two of the suspects were dead, but the third, Robert Hinton, was on his way to Melbourne aboard the SS *Te Anau* with the gold. He returned Nightingale to the stables and hurried across the street to the post office, whistling to himself.

18

Caroline's Father

Mette could scarcely contain her excitement. She had the gold, or at least some of it, and now Frank would be able to claim the reward. She did not know how much a gold ingot weighed, or even how one looked. The most gold she'd ever seen was a British Full Sovereign from the Royal Mint in Melbourne, which her sister Maren had shown her. Maren's husband had purchased five of them from the Bank of New Zealand in Palmerston North, one for each of their children. They looked beautiful, and were quite heavy, although light enough to carry around in your pocket. Maren had done that when she came to show them to Mette. The ingots must be a lot heavier than five gold sovereigns, but without knowing the weight of one, she couldn't guess how many were hidden in the bottom of the bag. But one, at the very least.

She walked up and down between the beds, hugging herself, trying not to wake the girls, wondering how much longer Frank would be. Every few minutes she stopped to stare out the window, hoping to catch a glimpse of him.

And finally, there he was, coming along the street with

another man. She couldn't see who the other man was, because all she could see the was tops of their heads. But the man in front was definitely Frank. She would recognize him anywhere.

For ten minutes she did not know where to put herself, hurrying to the door to listen for a knock, sitting on the bed to calm herself, then jumping up and running to the window; finally, she heard a soft tap. She moved the bag away from the door, but stopped herself from flinging it open, remembering Frank had asked her not to open the door for anyone. Her heart was pounding in anticipation of the surprise she had for him, but to show him she'd paid attention, she left the chain on the door and opened it a tiny fraction. Frank was standing outside in the hallway, his back to her. Or she thought it was Frank. There was something about him that did not quite look like Frank. His clothes were different. Had he taken the time to buy himself a new coat and boots? Was that why he'd rushed off from the stables so suddenly?

"Frank?" she said tentatively. He turned around.

Not Frank, but a tall, dark-haired man about the same size as Frank, although younger and beardless. He had a long, thin nose and narrow-set eyes that made him look cruel. She stared at him, and he stared back, his lips curving slowly into a smile.

"Is this her?" he asked someone standing just out of view.

The other person moved forward so she could see him. "Yes, that's her."

"Mr. Smith!" She had been sure he'd drowned, but here he was.

She slammed the door in the man's face, but before the lock could click into place, he raised his booted foot and stamped it hard against the door panels, splitting one with a loud crack as the door came off its hinges and the chain snapped.

The force knocked her back onto the bed beside Helen. Both the girls woke up, crying. The intruder strode into the room, stopped, and stared down at them, his eyes going from one to the other.

"Ah, as you said, Smith. There are two of them. Now, which is mine?"

Mr. Smith followed him into the room, looking around nervously as if he expected Frank to jump from the wardrobe. "I'm not sure, but I think the darker one is hers. The other one must be yours. I haven't seen that one before."

"Hmm." He eyed the girls, taking his time, looking from one to the other. "I think the darker one looks more like me. Are you sure she isn't mine?"

Mette threw her body across the cot, covering Sarah Jane. "She's mine, she's mine," she said. "Please don't take her away. The other one is yours, not this one."

"Aha," he said. "A double bluff, perhaps?" She could smell alcohol on his breath, and could see his pupils were dilated. He'd been drinking. "You're defending the wrong baby in hopes I'll take the other one instead of yours, aren't you? Clever girl."

Mette was confused. "What do you mean...?" She started to say, but he interrupted her.

"Tell you what, Smith. "Let's take both babies. We can always toss one away when we find which one is mine."

"No, no, please," said Mette. Frank would be terribly unhappy if she let this man take Helen, but she would do anything rather than have him take Sarah Jane. "I'll pay you if you let me keep both of them. I have gold. In the Gladstone bag. Lots of gold. Please take it. It's worth thousands of pounds. But leave my baby with me, and leave Helen as well."

"Who the devil is Helen?" he asked. "You mean Caroline?"

He strode over and picked up the Gladstone bag, almost losing his balance as he rounded the end of the bed. Perhaps if she delayed him until Frank returned, he would punish this evil man who thought throwing a baby away was reasonable.

"The bag is empty." He dropped the bag to his side.

"It has a false bottom," she said. "Please. Lift it up to the light and look inside. You'll see. There's gold in there."

He did as she asked, holding it to the window. "Ah, I can see something. An ingot perhaps. Barely worth my while."

"We'd better hurry up, Sir Charles. The husband will be back soon. I promise you, I saw him with the darker baby of the two, and it was definitely his. The other one is yours."

Sir Charles walked over to the bed where Helen was on her knees, swaying back and forth, trying to get one leg under herself so she could stand, but having no luck because of the softness of the bed. He crouched down beside her. "I don't give a damn about the husband. I'll handle him." He put his hand out to Helen and pinched her on the cheek. "Hello, Caroline. I'm your father. Would you like to come on a trip with me?" He winked at Mette. "I think I'll take this one. I see you're looking relieved, and I assume I now have the correct infant."

He picked her up. She frowned and asked, "Dada?"

"Yes," he said. "Dada. I can see we're going to get along famously. And don't worry about the gold, madam. This little lady is worth a thousand times any gold you might have in the bottom of your bag."

He took Helen — Caroline, not Helen, and Mette would have to get used to that — and swept from the room, followed by Mr. Smith. She waited until she heard him clumping down the stairs and ran to the landing, and screamed as hard as she could. She saw them go out through the front door and turn right.

Captain Scott hurried from his parlour on the lower floor and started up the stairs towards her. "What's going on? Is someone hurt?"

"Captain Scott, they've taken the baby, two men. A tall dark-haired man and another man in a light grey suit." It was as much description she could manage in a short time, and Captain Scott jumped into action, sprinting through the front door and out into the street. He stopped to look either way, and took off running in the direction of the stables.

She followed him at a safe distance. Other people who knew him would come to his assistance, and she wasn't going to get involved while she was holding Sarah Jane. The captain stopped abruptly outside the stables and went inside as if he'd spotted someone inside. Sir Charles, already astride a horse, erupted past him, slapped the horse on the rear, and took off at a gallop towards Stirling Point.

By the time she reached the stables, Captain Scott and a stable hand had wrestled Mr. Smith to the ground. They pulled him up, and, each holding an arm, dragged him back to the hotel. Mette followed, holding Sarah Jane tightly, her emotions in a swirl. What was Frank going to say about Helen being taken? What did Sir Charles whatsisname mean when he said his daughter was worth a thousand times more than the gold in the bottom of Mr. Hinton's bag? He definitely didn't mean he loved her so much she was worth more to him than gold — he was obviously talking about financial worth. He hadn't even recognized his own daughter.

"He doesn't know the Bluff, that chap," said Captain Scott as he manhandled Mr. Smith into the reception area. "He can't escape in that direction. He'll be back." He pulled Mr. Smith's arm behind his back and forced him into a straight-backed chair. The groom stood behind the captain, his arms crossed, making sure Smith could not leap to his feet and make a run for it.

"Right, young fellow." Captain Scott loomed over Smith, glaring down at him. "What have you got to say for yourself?"

"You won't catch him." Smith looked defeated. "He has a ketch waiting on the other side of the hill, near Lookout Point. He'll be out of the country within the hour."

"Can't you ask the police to stop him?" asked Mette.

"I could call out the volunteer rifles," said Captain Scott. "But not within the hour. And we have only one policeman stationed here. He's over at the lockup. He's a good chap, but he'd never manage to get across Bluff Hill to Lookout Point in an hour. He's a bit too fond of mutton bird and oysters, I'm sorry to say."

Mette stood in front of Mr. Smith, out of reach of his arms and feet. She didn't trust him at all now. "Can you please tell me what's going on? Is Sir Charles really Helen...I mean Caroline's father? And why does he want her so badly? Did he pay for the McNab's to kidnap her? And who are you, and how did you get involved in all of this?"

He sighed and stared at the floor for a few minutes. Mette had decided she wasn't going to get any answers from him, when he looked up at her and said sadly, "I'm finished, I suppose. What do you want to know?"

"Start by telling me who you are. Is your name really Smith?"

He nodded. "I'm the assistant to Caroline's great uncle, the Commissioner of Crown Lands for Otago."

"So you are an Assistant Commissioner," said Mette. "But

not for the police."

"I never claimed I was from the police," he said defensively. "Everyone just jumped to that conclusion. When Caroline was kidnapped, the commissioner was sure it was her father who had taken her. And we knew about the pair who had most likely done it for him, Betsy and William McNab, a brother and sister. He's ex-Indian Army, goes by the nickname of Whitey McNab, because of his hair. They've worked for him for years. I'd never seen them, but I'd heard them described as fair haired — very fair haired, in the way some British people are. When I saw you with the baby I was sure you were Betsy McNab. So I followed you. When you claimed your husband had gone down with the Tararua, I thought you were lying, and that you were really looking for your brother. So I came with you, and..."

"And you sent a telegram to the Commissioner before we left Wyndham." Everything was falling into place.

But Mr. Smith surprised her. "No. I never intended to take Caroline back to him. He's a cheapskate. I always meant to get her to Sir Charles. He has more to gain and would be more likely to reward someone who helped him. I sent him a telegram to let him know that the ship carrying his daughter had gone down, but that I had found her. I asked him to meet me in Bluff as soon as he could. I would wait for him in a lodging house I knew about. After I jumped into the river, I swam ashore at the bend in the river and walked down to Bluff."

"Why not work with William McNab, then? Why did you have to kill him?"

"That was an accident. I was trying to get him to tell me who had the real baby, once I knew there were two. He said your husband had rescued one after the wreck, and he thought she was Caroline. I didn't mean to hurt him, but he fought with me. I had no choice."

Captain Scott had been listening to the whole story with great interest. "Tell me," he said. "So I have the full picture here. Why was it so important for Sir Charles — what's his last name, by the way? — for sir Charles to be in possession of his daughter?"

"Pomeroy," said Smith. "Sir Charles Pomeroy. It's complicated…"

"Go ahead." Captain Scott folded his arms across his chest. "I'm listening."

"There's a woman," said Smith. "A very pretty woman. She lives in Dunedin under the care of my employer, her uncle. She used to work as a lady's maid for Sir Charles mother, at her place in Surrey. That's in England," he said to Mette, as if she didn't know anything about England. "And he impregnated her. She wasn't exactly willing, although she was just a maid, so it shouldn't have mattered."

"Of course it mattered. It always matters," said Mette sharply.

Both men glanced at her, puzzled, and then Smith continued. "The old woman — Sir Charles' mother — was very upset, and she cut him out of her will. She was the one with all the money. Her father made his money in coal mining. Her husband, Sir Charles father, had the title. And she left her entire fortune to Caroline, everything except the house, which belonged to Sir Charles' late father and was entailed to the male line."

Mette knew what was coming. She was half-way through Bleak House already. "Jarndyce v. Jarndyce," she said triumphantly. "Caroline was made a Ward of Chancery, like Ada and Richard."

Mr. Smith seemed to understand what she was talking about. "Yes, only I believe it's called Ward of the Court nowadays. Caroline is to receive everything when she turns eighteen. Until then, whoever has her in their care will have use of the money, on application to the Court of Chancery. Sir Charles was sure he would be treated fairly, as long as he had Caroline…"

"What's going on here?" asked Frank. He had come through the front door of the hotel looking pleased with himself, but his expression had changed as soon as he saw Mette and Mr. Smith.

"Sir Charles has taken Caroline," said Mette. "I'm sorry Frank, but I couldn't stop him. I even offered to give him the gold in exchange for her, but he refused, and now we know…"

"Who the bloody hell is Caroline?" he asked. "And what's this about the gold? Hinton has it. I just saw him leave for Melbourne on the *Te Anau*."

19

At Lookout Point

Nightingale seemed happy about being torn from the comfort of her stable for another ferocious ride so soon after Frank had left her there. She pranced out into the street as if she'd had a full day of rest, not merely twenty minutes, with Frank mounted on her, ready to run down the bastard who had taken Helen. Or Caroline, as he supposed he should call her, although she'd always be Helen to him.

He hadn't stopped to get the full story from Mette and Captain Scott, pausing just long enough to find out that Caroline had been kidnapped by her own father for financial reasons — something to do with Charles Dickens, seemingly, although he wasn't totally clear on that. But he knew he had to get her back. Mette had assured him that Caroline's father was a nasty piece of work who intended to squeeze all Caroline's money from her and then toss her aside. She'd said something about the gold reward, as well, but he'd put that out of his mind. The gold was with Hinton, he knew it was. And that reward was not important right now. All he had on his mind was that he had to rescue Caroline.

Captain Scott had directed him to ride through town and up onto Bluff Hill to the lookout station. From there he'd be able to see Lookout Point on the coast, where Pomeroy's boat was anchored. To get to the coast from the lookout he'd have to ride downhill through rocky scrubland, Captain Scott said, but he could follow tracks made by Maori, who had a camp in the area. Whether he'd be able to catch up to Pomeroy and rescue Caroline, he didn't know. But he was going to damn well try. He still had the gun Inspector Buckley have given him, and would shoot Pomeroy if he wouldn't return Caroline, even if it meant going to prison.

Nightingale took the track up to the lookout station at a gallop, navigating the rough ground with ease. At the top of the hill, the coast of Southland spread before him, from the sandy shoals off Tiwai Point across the channel, to Dog Island hunched down in the ocean to the south, and Lookout Point beneath him on the rocky shore of Foveaux Strait. From Lookout Point, a broad, stony strip ran along to a cove, where a ship's boat was docked beside a rickety wooden landing, unmanned. A small ketch, probably weighing no more than sixty tons, bobbed at anchor in the cove, its sails drooping, windless.

Wishing he had a telescope with him, he squinted down at the cove, and saw a dinghy carrying two men push off towards the ketch, one man rowing, the other sitting in the prow. He couldn't tell if Caroline was with him, but it had to be Pomeroy.

He found his way down to the shore with difficulty, Nightingale picking her way between the rocks and scrubby vegetation, while he kept his eye on the ocean to see what was going on with the ship. The dinghy reached its destination and the passenger passed a bundle to someone on board. Caroline, he was sure. The right size, anyway.

He reined Nightingale in, dismounted, and checked the ship's boat. It had come from a wreck, he suspected. The name *England's Glory* was evident on the prow, the paint fading. The boat was too large for him to handle by himself. He'd be lucky if he could even launch it. But under a cluster of stunted cabbage trees near the shore, he could see a man lying on his back, asleep. He left Nightingale and hurried over to him; a young man, a Maori, his hands crossed over his chest, snoring loudly.

"*Kia Ora.*" He nudged the sleeping man with his boot. Once, he'd been able to speak Maori reasonably well, but he'd forgotten most of it, and it always deserted him when he needed it most.

The man woke with a start and sat up, rubbing his eyes. "Yeah?"

"Is that your boat at the dock?"

"I was asleep."

"I'm sorry. But I need to get to that ketch. The passenger they picked up just now has kidnapped a young girl — taken her from her mother. I'd row out there by myself in the ship's boat by the dock, but I don't think I can."

The Maori stood up and stretched. "Yeah, we saw him come down the hill with the baby. He paid my brother to take the horse back to the Bluff. I can get another couple of blokes if you like." He stuck two fingers in his mouth and gave a piercing whistle. Two more young men, looking like copies of the first, rose like wraiths from the scrub.

"My brothers," said the first man. "That one is Kai and the other one is Nikau, like the palm tree. I'm Taika. Taika Korowhiti."

"Frank Hardy," said Frank. "You speak English very well." He glanced at the ketch. It hadn't moved. Becalmed by the look of it. He had some time.

"My mum's from Liverpool, isn't she?" said Taika. "They speak English there, don't they?"

"More or less," Frank agreed. "Listen, can you help me?"

"Can you pay?"

Frank took a pound note from his pocket. He had three more, and then he was done. "Would a quid be enough?"

Kai and Nikau approached and stood beside the boat, hands on hips, listening. They were big men, bigger than their brother, and strong looking. The forward line on a rugby team. Good in a fight, he was sure.

"Come on, Taika," said Kai. "Five minutes rowing for a quid? That's not bad."

"You'd have to wait around and row me back in," said Frank. He might be able to swim the distance with Caroline, but it would be risky.

"Will the bloke just give her to you?"

"It could involve a fight."

"Now you're talking," said Kai. "We haven't had a good punch up for a dog's age. What do you say, my brothers?"

"Alright, then," said Taika. "Let's do it. Give me the pound first, in case he shoots you or something."

They climbed into the ship's boat; Taika tossed him an oar. "You gonna have to paddle, man. Make it even so we don't go round in circles. Usually my other brother, Billy, is with us, but he took the horse back."

"What are you three — four — doing over here?" he asked, between pulls. "Do you live in this area?"

"*Titi*," said Taika. "That's mutton birds to you. We're from Invercargill, but we have an auntie in the Bluff."

191

"What about mutton birds?"

"It's harvest time, over on the island, late harvest. The young ones come out of their burrows at night and stretch their wings. Helps them grow, but makes it easy to catch them."

Frank had eaten mutton bird, a dark-brown bird about the size of a duck. He'd been told they acquired that name because they tasted like mutton, but he couldn't see it. Tasted like a bird to him, a duck, but more fatty than duck if that were possible.

"You've been over on Stewart Island harvesting mutton birds? Do you row across the Strait in that ship's boat?"

Taika took his time answering. They were almost at the ketch before he did. "We're not supposed to do it. Only Maori born on the island can harvest the *titi*, but the *titi* don't know that. And there's so many. It'd be a waste if we left them."

"I won't tell anyone if you don't mention that I'm taking the baby back to her mother. And I won't mention that you have this boat, either."

They grunted their agreement.

Three crewmen were leaning over the rail of the ketch watching their approach, one wielding a long boat hook. The pole was wavering, as if the man holding it was nervous. None of the three looked ready for a fight.

Kai stood on the seat of the ship's boat, got his balance with his feet apart and his arms out, and then leapt forward and grabbed on to the hook, swinging and grinning back at his brothers. "I'm going to pull him in. Watch." He looked up at the crewman. "Hope you can swim."

The man slid slowly across the rails, the other two crewmen gradually releasing their hold on his trousers. As he hit the water, his arms wide, he screamed and then stopped as the wind was knocked out of him. He turned on his front and struck out towards the shore, his head up, his arms splashing wildly.

"That's my one," said Kai. "Now you arseholes get yourselves one."

Taika and Nikau scrambled aboard the ketch and took on the two remaining crewmen, while Kai stayed in the boat, keeping it in place for the return. The combatants faced off, ignoring Frank, who grabbed hold of the ship's rope and swung himself on board. He pushed past the four men and went into the cabin.

"Fah!'

Caroline was sitting on Sir Charles Pomeroy's knee as he fed her grapes. He had a glass of something amber-coloured in one hand, and his eyes were half closed.

"I don't think you should be feeding her those," said Frank. "She'll choke."

Pomeroy set Caroline on the floor and rose languidly, swaying, his drink in his hand. "Is she always smelly like this?" he asked. "I assumed my daughter would be better perfumed."

His foolishness caught Frank off guard. "She needs to be…" he started to say.

Pomeroy sprang past Caroline, tossed his glass on the floor, and lunged at Frank, grabbing him by the throat. Frank fell back and twisted around, pushing away with his heels. For a drunk, the man had a lot of strength in his hands. He managed to loosen his grip, and approached Pomeroy in a defensive crouch, his elbows out, hands ready, moving from one foot to the other.

"I'm not going to be as easy as that dolt Smith." Pomeroy put up his fists like a bare-knuckle fighter. "I was a boxer at Eton. I still remember all the moves."

Frank was tired of old boys from English public schools telling him they had learned everything they knew at an elite school in Britain. He'd learned everything he knew about fighting in the army, and that training was much more brutal than anything Pomeroy might have learned at Eton.

He feinted towards Pomeroy, a left jab and a right, bare-knuckle style, and then side-stepped and stamped the side of Pomeroy's knee inwards, right at the joint. He heard a click and Pomeroy yelped and fell back onto the couch, clutching his knee to his chest. Out on the deck the Korowhiti boys were performing a thundering *haka*, a Maori war dance. They were trying to scare the crewmen, he knew. Secretly, most Europeans were terrified of Maori fighters. He heard a splash, followed by another as the crewmen jumped overboard.

Caroline had crawled over to the door, looking back at Frank to see if he was going to follow. Keeping one eye on her, he grabbed Pomeroy by his ears and jerked him to his feet, then threw him back again, bouncing his head against the wall. Pomeroy grabbed him between his legs and squeezed hard. Frank flinched and tried to pull himself away. Pomeroy was learning, but a bit late in the day. He got hold of Pomeroy's collar and pulled him upright. Pomeroy coughed once, let go of Frank's crotch, and head butted him. It wasn't a very successful head butt, but it did the job.

"Damn you." Frank could feel blood oozing from his nose. Time to get this finished. He wound up and delivered a haymaker right into the centre of Pomeroy's face. Pomeroy fell back onto the seat, blood gushing from his nose, dazed.

Frank flexed his fingers, hoping he hadn't broken any bones in his hand. "Next time you want to terrorize a woman alone with two babies, think twice." He looked around the cabin.

"Caroline?"

She was gone. He rushed outside in time to see her doing what she had almost done in the shearing shed a few short days ago. She was on her feet, tottering towards the the open gate; he lunged for her just as she walked through it and into the water. He heard a splash.

"Dammit, Caroline."

Frank leapt over the railing after her. She floated for a minute, her clothing billowing out around her head like a halo, and then sank slowly beneath the water, a surprised look on her face. He took a deep breath and plunged in the direction he'd last seen her.

For a long, agonizing minute, he could not find her. The water was murky, full of the sand and dirt it had picked up along the shore. He was bursting for air, ready to go up for a breath, when he felt the side of her head. Holding one of her ears, he kicked himself lower, got one arm around her chest, and swam to the surface, gasping for air, pushing her up first above his head so she would surface first.

"Are you alright Caroline?"

She coughed and said a weak, "Fah?"

"Thank god," he said.

"Hand her to me," said Kai, from somewhere above him.

He thrust her up into the boat, and dragged himself up after her. Taika and Nikau had followed him into the water, and they rolled across the gunnel, laughing happily.

"That was bloody good," said Nikau. "Any time you want to take us along on a fight, let us know."

Sir Charles Pomeroy was not done with them. He limped out onto the deck carrying a fowling piece that had probably been in his family for fifty years. Holding his gun straight out and pointed at Frank, he fired. The shot splashed in the water around the boat. Frank reached for his gun, knowing it might not fire after being in the water, but Taika beat him to it, bending down and opening a box underneath his seat. "Here, brothers." He took one rock, and another, and another, piling them by his feet. His brothers picked up the stones and lobbed them at Pomeroy, who withdrew to the safety of his cabin amidst a flurry of sea gulls that rose from the water, screeching, and surrounded the ketch.

He peered out through the doorway, and said, "I'll get you Hardy. I'll send the full force of the law after you. I went to school with the Commissioner of Police. I'll write him a strong letter as soon as I get back to England."

Frank hugged Caroline, laughing. "I've got a few months of freedom, then," he said to the Korowhiti boys. "Lucky for me he hasn't heard of the telegraph." He took off Carolyn's napkin, shook it out into the water and folded it back around her with the pilch holding it in place, mentally thanking Mrs. Brunton.

"Best I can do, sorry," he said to her. "Now, let's get you home to your mother."

She smiled up at him. "Fah."

20

Rewarded

Frank decided that as long as Colonel Roberts was covering expenses, they would stay in a decent hotel and eat well. He inquired at the station and was directed to the Royal George Hotel on George Street, conveniently located a short distance from the North Ground, where Caroline had been kidnapped by the McNabs during a game of cricket, and therefore close to the home where she lived with her mother and her mother's uncle, Mr. Smith's employer.

Mette was ecstatic when they arrived at the luxurious hotel, which she decided was even better than Captain Scott's hotel in Bluff. She especially liked the fact that it was wedged between the Glasgow Pie House and Ready Money Richards, the latter a shop that sold high quality goods for low prices. She was determined to buy a nice frock for Sarah Jane at the Ready shop, because she was growing so fast. She still had ten shilling left, and she thought that would buy Sarah Jane a frock and some booties, with change enough for a coffee and a piece of pie at the pie house. That would keep the two of them occupied while Frank returned the gold ingot to the Bank of New Zealand,

and Caroline to her mother, both of which Mette decreed he should do by himself.

He started with the Bank of New Zealand, a few blocks south of the hotel on George Street. Six months earlier, men from the bank had delivered eleven boxes of gold ingots to the *SS Tararua.* Shortly after — no one was quite sure when — one of the boxes containing five ingots had been stolen by Hinton and his gang. Somehow or other, someone had brought the gold back to Dunedin with the intention of transferring it to Australia one ingot at a time. How much had already gone to Australia, or elsewhere, was unclear. Inspector Buckley suspected it could have gone to America, but he had no proof.

The reward offered by the bank was a thousand pounds. How much of that could he expect for recovering one ingot and fingering Hinton as the guilty party. Knowing bankers, the smallest amount they could get away with, but he should have some cash coming to him. If they didn't give him at least a hundred quid he would create a fuss.

He was ushered in to the office of the assistant manager, a balding, middle-aged man wearing the same dark grey suit and embroidered waistcoat bankers wore throughout the colony and sporting a pair of gold-framed spectacles on the bridge of his nose.

The assistant manager got right to the point. "Colonel Roberts contacted us saying you've retrieved part of our bullion."

Frank set Caroline on a wing chair beside the desk and opened his haversack. He placed the ingot on the assistant manager's desk, where it sat, gleaming richly.

The assistant manager picked it up and turned it over,

checking to see if the hallmark was correct, using his spectacles as a magnifying glass. "Yes. This is our gold. Thank you for returning it, Sergeant Hardy. What a pity there's only the one ingot."

"My wife saw Hinton, the thief, going into a house on Moray Place," said Frank. "I told Colonel Roberts about that in my telegram." His second telegram, of course, the one he'd sent after Mette had finally showed him the Gladstone bag with the false bottom that opened with the key he'd found on Sampson, and he'd understood that when he'd seen Robert Hinton sailing off on the *Te Anau* with a bag by his feet, the bag had contained a large, boring manuscript.

"The police have already raided that house," said the assistant manager. "They found nothing, unfortunately. The woman who owns the house rents out rooms. Hinton has been staying there regularly, always in the same room. She thinks he may have hidden the gold under the floorboards or in the walls. The bank inspectors pulled the room apart, but found nothing, as I said."

"Did you arrest Hinton when he disembarked in Melbourne?"

The assistant manager laid the gold ingot back on his desk, replaced his spectacles and looked at Frank. "For what? All he had on him was a very large manuscript. He was as surprised to see it as the police were. And of course, they couldn't arrest him for having a manuscript with him, even though it clearly did not belong to him. It wasn't as if he was trying to claim he'd written it. If he had, we could have arrested him under the copyright laws."

"What happened to the manuscript?"

The assistant manager shrugged. "I have no idea. The

Melbourne Constabulary tossed it in the rubbish, I should imagine."

Frank sighed and picked up Caroline. "I believe there's a reward?"

"We'll contact Colonel Roberts about that. I'm sure there'll be something, but not the full amount, of course. Nothing close to it. Perhaps a small emolument to show our appreciation?"

He went next to the house on Cumberland Street where Caroline's mother lived with her uncle, Mr. James Graham. He'd learned from Inspector Buckley that she'd come to New Zealand to escape Sir Charles, and had taken shelter with her uncle James, who had arrived several years earlier and made a success of himself, working his way up to the post of Commissioner of Crown Lands for Otago. Unfortunately for him, he'd taken on a young Englishman named Roderick Smith as his assistant.

The house was a modest verandah villa, with attractive lace curtains and a door painted bright red. He knocked and waited. He did not know what to expect of Caroline's mother, but hoped she'd be happy to see her daughter returned. While anyone would be better than Sir Charles Pomeroy, he dearly wanted Caroline to have a happy life.

The door opened and a woman wearing a small cap and a floral morning gown opened the door. She looked so much like Caroline it took his breath away: small, energetic, with bright blue eyes that were rimmed with red, as if she'd been crying.

She clapped her hands to her mouth, then reached for her daughter.

"Oh, Caro, my darling Caro."

"Mama?' Caroline held out her arms out towards her mother. "Mama?"

Frank set Caroline on her feet on the verandah, and watched her mother's eyes open in surprise as her daughter toddled forward. She swooped her up and held her in a crushing embrace, crying and laughing at the same time. "The precious wee thing can walk." He noticed she had a strong Scottish accent. "When did she start to walk?"

Frank wasn't going to tell her about the night in the shearing shed, so said instead, "A week ago at the home of Mr. and Mr.s Brunton, not far from Fortrose. It took me by surprise as well. She's very young to be walking."

"She'll be one year old in three weeks. I know she's small for her age but she's very lively and active."

"So I discovered," said Frank. "I've been carrying her around for a week and she's been a proper handful."

She smiled. "Please come in. My uncle, Mr. Graham, would like to speak with you. He's heard the whole story from the police and he'd like to thank you personally."

Frank wanted to make sure Caroline's home was a proper place for her, so he followed her mother into the house. A short, rotund older man who reminded him of Tweedledum or Tweedledee in *Through the Looking Glass* was seated at a desk in the parlour. He rose from his chair and shook Frank's hand with both of his.

"Sergeant Hardy, thank you for bringing our little angel home. We can't thank you enough."

"Happy to do it," said Frank. "I learned a few things about baby girls in the past week that will come in handy. I have a daughter of my own."

"The same age?" asked Caroline's great uncle.

"A few months younger," said Frank. "But the same size."

"Not surprising, considering the size of her father. Now, Helena will bring you a cup of tea while we talk, won't you Helena?"

Frank grinned to himself. Something had led him to use the name Helen for Helena's daughter. Perhaps it was divine intervention. Or perhaps she'd answered to that name when she was about to step from the loft because she recognized it.

Helena left and he could hear her in the next room, humming to herself as she put a kettle on the hub. He heard her say, "Careful, Caroline," and smiled. Caroline would never be careful.

"Now, Sergeant, first I have to apologize for Mr. Smith, my former assistant. I hear he caused you some trouble?"

Frank nodded. "He'll be paying for it for a long time, I imagine. Will they send him back here to gaol?"

"I believe so. The Dunedin Gaol isn't far from here, on the corner of Castle Street by the Law Courts. I'll visit him, of course. I hope he escapes hanging. I disapprove of hanging. We've only had three in Dunedin, the last one a year ago — a Chinese fellow who was falsely convicted, I believe. But they hanged him anyway. Ah Lee, the poor chap's name was. Hanged because he was Chinese, and so was the real murderer."

Helena served tea and sat down across from Frank, with Caroline on her knee. She wriggled off and toddled over to him. "Fah?"

"She's trying to say Frank." He took her hand in his and squeezed it. "Caroline, I'm going to miss you. But I have to return to my own little girl."

"Before you go, I have something for you. A small reward for rescuing our darling girl from the ocean."

Twice, Frank thought, although he thought it prudent not to say. Not to mention the time she almost walked into space in the shearing shed. If she was a cat she would already have used several of her nine lives. Caroline's uncle went to his desk and picked up a piece of paper. He put it into an envelope and handed it to Frank. A bank draft, Frank suspected. He refrained from tearing open the envelope to check. He wasn't expecting much. Mr. Smith had said the uncle was a cheapskate. He'd look when he got back to the hotel. Not that it mattered. He cared a lot more about returning Caroline than he did about being paid for it. He would have turned it down if he hadn't needed the money.

He returned to the hotel and found Mette lying on the bed with Sarah Jane, reading the Dunedin paper. They looked contented, and it did his heart good. Sarah Jane was resting against Mette's hip, chewing a red bootie she had pulled from her foot.

"Were they nice people?"

"Very nice," he said. "I was happy to leave Caroline with them. As long as that idiot Pomeroy doesn't return, she'll be alright. I told her mother if she and Caroline are ever in Wellington they can stay with us. I'd like to think that Caroline and Sarah Jane will be friends one day."

"And did the bank manager give you a thousand pounds?"

He pulled James Graham's bank draft from his pocket. "No. He's letting Colonel Roberts break the bad news to me. It won't be much. But Caroline's great uncle gave me something." He scanned the draft. "A hundred guineas. Not bad. At least we won't be totally broke for a few months."

"I've been thinking about what I should say to Professor

Mann," said Mette. "About his manuscript."

"What did you decide?"

She stared down at Sarah Jane, resplendent in a cream-coloured frock with a red bow on the back and little red booties, one on her foot, the other in her mouth. "Well, you know how I believe it's always best to tell the truth. Honesty is very important to me."

He knew her well. "So you're going to lie to him?"

Her face went pink and she nodded, still not looking at him. "I'm going to tell him a man I met in Dunedin has taken it to Melbourne."

"But that's true, isn't it?"

"Well, yes it is, but I'll imply that he's taking it to a publisher there, and that it may be a long time before he hears from the publisher."

"By the time he starts to wonder where it is, we'll be back on the farm." Frank sat on the bed beside her and picked up Sarah Jane. "You look very pretty. Your Mama has you all dressed up. Would you like to go to dinner?"

Mette sat up. "Dinner? What do you have in mind?"

"I stopped at the dining room downstairs just now. They have an excellent dinner tonight. Oyster soup, followed by a choice of roast beef and Yorkshire pudding or freshly caught snapper on a bed of rice, and for vegetables, asparagus, green peas, or artichokes. Treacle pudding for desert."

"Can we afford that?"

Frank pulled out his last two pounds. "This is all I've got left. Just enough for a decent meal and a couple of drinks. I've got our return tickets already, thanks to Colonel Roberts, and Nightingale is being shipped to Wellington tomorrow on the *Hawea.*"

"Isn't Colonel Roberts paying all our expenses?"

Frank returned his last two pounds to his pocket. "I'll see what they say downstairs. Worth a try. If they go for it we'll have a feast. If not we can share the roast beef."

The maitre d'hotel was happy to send the bill to the Wellington Constabulary. Frank ordered the roast beef and Mette the fresh snapper.

"This is so nice," she said as she picked at the bones of the fish. "I wish we could eat like this all the time."

"One of these days, we will" he said. "I feel as if success is just around the corner. I'd like to be able to afford everything you want. I wish you'd bought yourself a new frock, and not just one for Sarah Jane."

She put down her fork. "I'm perfectly happy as we are. The main thing is we're all alive, after everything we went through. That's more than the passengers of the *Tararua* can say. So many dead."

"Do they know the final count yet?" he said. "It must have been quite a few."

"Well over a hundred," she said. "Perhaps as many as a hundred and thirty. I was reading a report of the inquest in the paper when you returned."

"I suppose they found Captain Garrard responsible," said Frank. "The poor bastard."

"You'll have to stop swearing like that." said Mette. "I keep finding myself doing it as well, and I don't want to. It's not ladylike."

He grinned at her. "Neither is throwing someone off the back of a wagon. But you're right. I'll try not to. Not in front of you, anyway. What else did you learn from the inquest?

Where's it being held? In Dunedin?"

"Wyndham. Mrs. Brunton's son Charles is on the jury. Inspector Buckley's there as well. They don't have a final account of the number of people who died, because bodies are still coming ashore all along the coast."

"What about Captain Garrard, then. What did they say about him?"

"Mr. Malone testified that Captain Garrard did everything he could to keep the passengers safe and hopeful. He said he made sure the boats were put off with the best crews possible on each one. He must have known you'd be a good crew member, don't you think?"

"I'd like to think so," said Frank.

She reached over and squeezed his hand. "He made a good choice. And so did I."

21

Home Again

Professor Mann was delighted. "My manuscript has gone to a publisher in Melbourne?" His top lip twitched with excitement. "I never imagined…I knew it was…was *sehr gut*, but…a publisher, after so many years. *Das ist wunderbar!*"

Mette disliked having to lie to him, but what else was she to do? Break his heart with the truth? She had heard that a publisher might spend months, or even years, considering a manuscript, and then not return it when he decided against publishing it. At least this way the professor had something to look forward to. She had made up an elaborate story about a publisher's agent in Dunedin who had seen the manuscript and taken it with him back to Melbourne. She had almost put the fictional agent on the *Tararua*, but decided that was too much. No need to drown a fictional person if she could help it. Instead, she had emphasized that he was a forgetful, distracted sort of person, but she was sure that eventually he would contact the professor.

"That's wonderful news," he said. "I do need something to show to my department at the university, however. Did you have anything at all? The abstract, perhaps? The list of references?"

"Actually, I translated the abstract when I was on the train," said Mette.

He looked puzzled and she knew she had made an error. If she had the manuscript on the train, how did she give it to someone in Dunedin? She thought quickly. "I translated some of it on the way into Dunedin on the train, and then did some more in my hotel room before I met the agent." She opened her purse. "Here it is."

He took the pages from her. "This will be enough to secure my employment at the university," he said. "All they ever read is the abstract, in my experience. And the thought that someone is considering publishing my opus will spur me to write more on the topic."

"If you write anything new, please consider me to do the translation." Deep down, she hoped he would never write anything again and certainly not ask her to translate it. She guessed that once he was fully employed at the university he would not. But they were still short of money and if she could find work it would help.

"Thank you, I may do that." He frowned. "I do have some work for you in the near future, however."

She waited, apprehensive. Please, no more boring texts to translate.

"A student of mine, a very good student, has been studying German and keeps asking me for extra tutoring. Perhaps you would like to help? The student comes from a very wealthy farm family in the Wairarapa and would pay well."

From there, everything fell beautifully into place.

The farm manager contacted Frank to say he'd sold a yearling, and had also leased out the lower portion of the farm for grazing. That gave them enough for Niall's quarterly stipend and for the next quarter's rent of their cottage in Wellington.

Frank met Colonel Roberts at the barracks and learned he was to receive a reward of seventy eight pounds, ten shillings and sixpence; the reward for a single ingot of the five stolen was two hundred pounds, but because he had not managed to implicate Robert Hinton in the robbery, the bank was paying him half that amount. Colonel Roberts presented him with the reward and a list of expenses he had deducted from the reward: the hotels, the train fares, the cost of transporting Nightingale from Bluff Harbour to Wellington, and all meals, including the large and delicious plate of Bluff Oysters they had eaten before they left Bluff.

All together, including the hundred guineas from Caroline's great uncle, they now had almost two hundred pounds, and both of them had work. They felt rich.

Joey returned from his grandmother's place in Palmerston North and they met him at the train station. Much to Joey's surprise, Frank picked him up and hugged him. He hugged Frank back and then wriggled out of his hold. "I missed you, Mumma," he said to Mette. "And you as well, Sergeant Frank. Please don't go away again for a while."

They sat on the verandah of their cottage and looked out over Wellington Harbour as the sun set late in May. Winter was coming on, but the day was unseasonably warm. Frank had one more surprise for her. He took out a letter and passed it to her.

"Look who's coming to New Zealand to visit us."

"Just tell me, who?"

"My father," he said. "He says he's tired of Gladstone and prison reform and all the wars Britain is fighting in Africa, and the suffragists and he wants to see if New Zealand is any better."

Mette was puzzled. "I thought Gladstone was the name of a bag. Your bag, in fact, the one I exchanged with Mr. Hinton."

He laughed. "I think the man came first, followed by the bag. William Gladstone, the Prime Minister, used to carry a bag of that style, so people started calling it a Gladstone bag."

"It will be interesting to meet your father," she said. "He sounds like a man with strong opinions."

"Yes," said Frank. "And not afraid to voice them to all and sundry."

The sun slipped below the hills across the harbour, and the water turned pink, silhouetting Somes Island on the far side. She leaned against Frank, happy. What would the next few months bring? She'd been hoping for another child soon, but that had not happened. Maybe the fates had planned something more exciting for them in the next year?

-THE END-

Thank you for reading the latest entry in *The Sergeant Frank Hardy Mysteries*. If you've written a review for one of my other books, thank you very much. You might be surprised to learn that reviews really help an author sell books (something to do with algorithms). I hope you'll consider leaving a review for *Come to Grief*. This book required an unusual amount of hard work and concentration as it took place during a historical disaster that I wanted to present as accurately as possible.

I read all the reviews, especially those with three or more stars! And I frequently make changes to my books based on readers' comments. You may have noticed, for example, that there are fewer Maori place names and Maori speakers in the newer books. In this book I gave the Korowhiti boys a mother from Liverpool, so Frank didn't have to use his poor Maori language skills to communicate with them. I loved creating those boys, by the way. I grew up with boys like that in Waitara and Patea.

If you'd like to hear about the next book, follow me on, BookBub or Twitter (@profwendy). I'm planning a book set on Somes Island, the quarantine island in Wellington Harbour, during a measles outbreak. Frank's father will also make his first appearance in the series, which you may have guessed.

Wendy

22

Real or Fictional?

While the other suspects were my own inventions, Robert Hinton was a real person and was a suspect at the time. One of the ingots was discovered after his death in Melbourne in 1883, but the other four were never recovered. He did not have a manuscript with him; Professor Mann and his opus were also inventions. As a writer who has twice lost manuscripts in computer crashes, I can identify with Professor Mann's loss. Think how difficult it must have been when there was only one copy of a book? Thomas Carlyle's maid accidentally burned the first volume of his three volume work on *The French Revolution*. In the novel and the various movies of Louisa May Alcott's *Little Women*, Amy March deliberately burns her sister Jo's manuscript.

Another interesting person was George Lawrence, who swam for help. He was very young — twenty-two. You can read about him and his subsequent life in an article in The Prow at http://www.theprow.org.nz/people/george-lawrence/#.YE_nbi296RZ. The article also features a painting of the sinking of the *SS Tararua*.

Mrs. Brunton was real, but became a fictional character to me when she rode Nightingale into Fortrose. She died in February 1888, aged 68:

> *The late Mrs Brunton was interred in Fortrose cemetery on the 7th inst., when a large number of relatives and residents assembled to pay their last respects to the departed. The deceased lady's illness was a protracted one, borne with Christian resignation and fortitude, and of her it may be truly said her end was peace. Southland Times, 15 February 1888.*